A REVOLUTIONARY WOMAN

A Revolutionary Woman

Sheila Fugard

GEORGE BRAZILLER · NEW YORK

Published in the United States in 1985
by George Braziller, Inc.
Copyright © 1983 by Sheila Fugard

First published in South Africa
by AD. Donker (Pty) Ltd 1983
and in Great Britain by Virago Press Limited 1984

Library of Congress Cataloging in Publication Data

√ Fugard, Sheila.
A revolutionary woman.
I. Title.
PR9369.3.F84R4 1985   823   85-3808
ISBN 0-8076-1127-1

Printed in the United States of America
First edition
Text design by Joe Marc Freedman

For Athol

"Sages say the path is narrow, and difficult to tread, narrow as the edge of a razor."
Katha Upanishad

Author's note

I have taken the liberty of using the real life characters of Gandhi and Kasturbai in a fictional manner. I hope that I will be forgiven any misrepresentation.

CONTENTS

PART ONE

A Revolutionary Woman

I return home. I shut the door and keep out the darkness. My house is a sanctuary, and I hold out against the Goths and Vandals of history. My books are my civilization; Sappho; the Odes of Horace; Greek plays; Elizabethan verse; Dante; Lao-tzu; the *Bhagavad Gita*; the Upanishads; Byron; Keats; Shelley; *Anna Karenina*; *War and Peace*; Ruskin; Christina Rossetti; Elizabeth Barrett Browning; Darwin's *Voyage of the Beagle*; and, recently, Virginia Woolf, and George Bernard Shaw.

I talk of the lives of others. I am fertilized, but not fulfilled, and my life insists on its own voice. The palimpsest is here in the Karoo. My life still rages as I recall it now.

Gandhi led a protest march, and we assaulted the Asiatic Office. It was winter in Johannesburg, and the mine dust blew. There was a sound of horse-drawn trams. The Mounted Police rode in, and there was a baton charge. I remember the mad eyes of the horses and their hot agonized breath and flaring nostrils. They trampled some of the protesters, and I still hear those cries even now. The same wounds fester here, only the air is more claustrophobic.

I have other memories too. I lived at the Phoenix settlement,

Gandhi's *ashram* in Natal. I gathered shells on a beach. It was a balmy day, and there was a cool fragrance. I recall that the frangipani trees flowered, and the pawpaws ripened, while the honeysuckle gave off its scent. I offered my shells to Gandhi. He received them graciously, and his nimble fingers fashioned a fan. Then, he took up another shell of his own, and blew on this conch. He roused heaven and earth, and other beings appeared and crowded the skies. These were the gods and goddesses of Hindu mythology; the dancing Shiva, with flowing hair; Kali, the dark mother, who holds a sword; Hanuman, the monkey god; Ganesh, the elephant god; the mythical *garuda* birds and the wise *naga* serpents. They all floated in space. Gandhi led that procession, and the *satyagrahis* followed him. These were the Indian passive resisters, and they believed in the sublime doctrine of *ahimsa*. This was the holy vision of those passive resisters as they celebrated the ideal of a classless society.

I remember that Kasturbai brought the tea. She came to disturb, with an angry face, as she frowned and recognized no visions. She does the household tasks. She touched the fan, and I saw my attempt at creating beauty fall apart as the shells broke. We gathered up the pieces together. Our eyes met as woman to woman, and our understanding grew. This was Gandhi's wife, and I was his disciple. I know that he's a difficult husband, and their marriage baffles me. She is the obedient wife. Gandhi's voice still summons me.

I remain here in New Kimberly, this isolated Karoo *dorp*. I hold a handful of sesame seeds. My fingers touch a truth. One seed is a hoe, and another is a spade, and still another is an axe. Other seeds are virtuous actions. Another is the mind's sharp eye. One seed contains the pith. This seed holds Gandhi's teachings and contains his voice. This is the truth of *ahimsa*, the doctrine of non-violent passive resistance. Gandhi fights oppression everywhere, the Boers in South Africa, and the British in India.

The sesame seeds insist. They rattle in my palm, and sounds

emanate from them. They speak in loud voices, with the grumblings of peasants, and the anger of the oppressed. They chant a familiar refrain and it's like a marching song. The tune is always the same, and I whistle it now. LIBERATION is being free of the Boer community . . . Charl Myburg . . . Jan Volschenk . . . Basie Viviers . . . Piet Burger . . . Andres Perreira . . . Wim Pieterse . . . Kobus le Grange . . . Ben Potgieter . . . Piet Barnard . . . Frans du Plessis . . . Willem Goosen . . . Petrus Nel . . . LIBERATION is being free of the Boers.

Racism is enshrined here. The Boers are the Brahmins, and the Coloureds are our Untouchables. The caste system of South Africa does exist, and it's simpler than in India. It's got to do with color, while in India, it's a complex ancestry, dating back to the beginnings of civilization. It's a thread that ramifies, a tapeworm in the bowels of India. Nobody can unravel it, even though Gandhi tries. He teaches at Sabarmati, the *ashram* in India. It's close to Ahmedabad, one of the great cities, and he will raise this ancient town to new heights. He fights for caste equality, and Gandhi has adopted an Untouchable family. He's taken in the pariahs of India, and their daughter has become his precious child. Ahmedabad will no longer be called the "city of dust." The ancient town regains its distinction. Sabarmati is close to the city; the *ashram* comprises a cluster of huts. There's a grove of trees, the river where Indian women pound their laundry flows nearby. They pummel cloth against rock, and the sacred cows wade there, and the mud oozes. Gandhi spins cloth, and Kasturbai stirs the pots. She wears a yellow sari and her face is composed. Ahmedabad's factories are close by and the city will surrender. The situation is rather like this dorp. There are prosperous houses here too. Our dorp is under cultivation, and sheep and goats are herded. Yet, poverty dominates the location. The Coloureds are our Untouchables, and they are the pariahs of the Karoo. Brahmin Boers rule here. It won't last forever: revolution changes everything.

The fire of the Karoo dawn is awesome. The red light of the

sky and earth insist that the Boer War is not over. I recall another dawn at the Phoenix settlement in Natal. Gandhi sat in the refectory, and his head was shaven like a monk's. He carried a bamboo staff, the trident of Shiva. He harmed no one, and righted an overturned beetle, and avoided a colony of ants. His skin had a dark patina, and his skull was a crinkled walnut. He hid nothing, thoughts were pure in their intention. His ears were large, and bright eyes were hidden behind spectacles. He scooped rice onto my plate, and then dipped his own vegetables into a bowl of goat's milk. I am still a follower of Gandhi, and a child of Tolstoy.

An eagle turns in the sky, as if the bird has fallen out of the immensity of space. I go out into the street, and the wind assaults me. The sky is a dome of white light, and the Lootsberg mountains are snow-covered. The dorp is under cultivation, and it's an oasis against drought, as well as an old bastion against a Kaffir attack, and a defiance against the British. The houses are white-washed and the green shutters are drawn. Poplars line the streets. The lucerne is green in the fields, and sheep crop grass. The Boers are prosperous. Thorn trees and dark rock are distant, and paths twist away from the dorp, and lead out across the veld. Another path winds toward the location. A chasm divides Boer and Coloured, and they are truly Brahmin and Untouchable.

Smoke comes from houses, and cattle in the distance crop scanty stubble. I meet Wim Pieterse, a neighbor, who is a wool merchant. His Dutch refinement lends him a lanky grace. The vision of the Amstel has been replaced by the Lootsberg, and he now survives in this intractable world. He speaks.

"We Boers have a feeling for the land. We have fought our own battles, the Kaffir wars and also the British imperialists and we will go on fighting if necessary."

Wim Pieterse talks out of a man's experience. He is also an Afrikaner now, and wonders if I will understand, because I am a woman, and English-speaking. He regrets that no quickening life stirs in my womb, and thinks me barren, and therefore clever. I answer.

"I think I understand . . ."

He looks toward the Lootsberg, and perhaps he does see the Kaffir hordes moving like a dark cloud on the horizon. He may even remember a British cavalry charge, when officers wielded bared sabres. The dark rock rises behind us and the distant thorn trees appear to intertwine. He turns to me, and asks:

"Why do you stay on?"

"I teach. I work at the Coloured school."

Wim Pieterse frowns. He would rather ignore the dorp's Untouchables. He is a member of the privileged class, a Brahmin Boer. He nods, and walks on.

I remember an errand, and hurry to the butcher's shop, where the carcasses hang from hooks, and a pig's head has glassy eyes. Jan Volschenk is like a berserk king in a Greek play. He raises that meat cleaver, another mad Oedipus swearing at the gods. Lights and livers slither about, as if they possess their own reptilian life, and sausages spill out like human intestines. His shop is a battlefield. I forget my errand and turn away, but he is importunate, and insists.

"A leg of lamb? Calfs liver? Succulent pork?"

I shake my head, and he grabs a pound of sausages, and flings them before me like a precious necklace. He slaps down lambs' kidneys that burst like black olives. Finally, I allow him to wrap up a chicken. The butcher lifts the meat cleaver, and splits a carcass in two. Then, he hands me my parcel and whispers,

"Be careful, Juffrou."

His words baffle me, and I leave the shop bewildered. I ponder Jan Volschenk's warning, and it makes no sense at all. Outside, the wind is sharp, and clouds move across the Lootsberg. I look toward the foothills and see that the *bywoners* supervise the laborers as they lay out the rows of tobacco plants. Our Untouchables are already at work, and the plants follow the land's natural contour.

I enter the trading store. Kobus le Grange, the auctioneer, and Frans du Plessis, the locksmith, drink coffee, and Piet Burger unpacks a chest of tea. These men appear uncomfortable in my presence. I recognize them, as Frans Hals, the artist, has painted similar merchants, and greed and pride mark the features of such men. Frans du Plessis is manipulative. He is like a spider, with a bulging body, and long arms and legs. Kobus le Grange is less evasive, as he slips hands into pockets, and puffs clouds of smoke. Piet Burger is most cautious, and affirms the counter, between us, as a no-man's land. There is a silence, and I hear an icicle fall from the roof. Piet Burger speaks:

"The winter's been cold. The drought makes it a harsh season."

Kobus le Grange is also severe, and echoes this gloom.

"Business is bad, and the wool clip is poor. Nobody has any money."

Frans du Plessis is dramatic, and hints at disaster.

"We can expect locusts to darken our skies. Beaufort West suffered and our turn is next."

I ignore these dire predictions, and collect my purchases. These men are concealing facts, and I'm not fooled. I walk out into the street. Charl Myburg paces in his garden. He is a competent Greek scholar, and a retired school teacher. Now he wrestles with Plato and Aristotle and mouths Greek quotations, even though their meaning eludes him. He avoids greeting me, and turns his back, and marches away. He's a sage who confronts bare branches, and I give him up. Let him talk to the clouds, or question the thorn trees. He'll find that silent rock is a formidable audience. I walk on alone, and frost cracks the earth. Spring is still some weeks away, and then the renewal will begin, with blossom on the trees.

A man runs past, and he is followed by a dog. This is Willem Goosen, and he's ill at ease with people. But he's happy running now. His eyes are downcast, and he observes the cracks in the mud, or spots a dung beetle. His feet hammer on the stones.

He is one with nature and looks past me toward the veld, and sees right to the heart of mountains. I make no attempt to halt his run. But the dog barks suddenly, as if it will tell all, and this animal will inform on the dorp's conspiracy. Then, I will discover why I am hated, ignored and slighted. The dog barks again, but I learn nothing, and the sound of it carries. The running man and the dog are soon out of sight. It's too late, and I've lost my chance. The cold earth cracks about me.

The cold bestows a radiance, and objects stand out clearly, as if they possess their own secret life. Trees precipitate their own green awareness of spring, and the clouds flock together and form a shore, while the sky is just another vast ocean. Andres Perreira approaches. He's a European, a man of Portuguese ancestry. He cannot have forgotten the sun-drenched patios, or the white stucco walls and the baroque churches with their serene madonnas and holy grottoes, or the cool Lisbon nights. He speaks politely, like a gentleman.

"Miss Ransome, it's cold weather. You should be indoors."

"The weather doesn't bother me. People are my problem."

Andres Perreira is not provoked, as he climbs onto his wagon. He is no proud *conquistador*, but just another member of the working class. He'd be better off picking olives, or bottling wine in Oporto. He flicks a whip, and I see the oxen move off. The Karoo will test him, and he will need to endure this drought.

I hear branches crack under wind, and distant thunder rolls now with a sound similar to stampeding animals. The wind flattens the scrub, and the veld gleams. Ben Potgieter and Basie Viviers approach me. Ben is the clever engineer, who erects the farm dams, and he's proved that bricks and mortar succeed against clay and rock. His dams hold precious water. The men raise their hats in greeting, yet they are critical and think me a high-handed woman. Ben Potgieter is quick-witted and speaks with a rare fluency.

"There is still no rain, Miss Ransome. It's fallen in other places . . . Pearston . . . Colesburg . . . and Jansenville, but we've seen none of it. The long summer will force an acknowledgment. Drought is like a cancer, and there are no hidden tumors. The disease is full-blown. The cattle are infected, and they dwindle, and die. We shrink too, and our vision becomes distorted."

Basie Viviers nods in agreement and comments: "It's true. This will be a long, hot summer. There's no end in sight to this drought, and it will simply go on. That's the truth."

These men stand like emissaries of gloom, and I must refute their words.

"It's the rot inside people. It's more severe than the drought. Lies and deceit are ugly, worse even than tumors and disease."

Ben Potgieter almost relents. I may remind him of a sister, or even a daughter, but then his expression hardens, and he sees me as just another cipher. I too am expendable, like the Untouchables in the location.

The Karoo is all space. The trees fail to fill the emptiness, and the fences are useless too. The Karoo swallows up everything; Brahmins and Untouchables, the flocks of sheep and goats, as well as the houses and possessions. There is much to contend with here.

I return home. I shut the door and keep out the darkness. My house is my sanctuary, and I hold out against the Goths and Vandals. My books are my civilization, and photographs of Gandhi and Kasturbai smile upon me. I am never entirely alone, even in this silted ocean, the Karoo, when the storm wracks this land, and I founder like a castaway. Kasturbai does not fail me. She is a dark Kali, and lends me her sword of wisdom. Then, I sever my attachment, and I too am radiantly pure. Gandhi proclaims the virtue of *ahimsa*. He is the Mahatma, a sage, who instructs the multitude, and is like a sun rising over India. I am no longer an absent child, lost in Africa. The continent of India, and that struggle, inform me here.

The doorbell rings, Petrus Nel is my caller. He's a military man and a Boer War *kommandant*. He refuses a chair, and chooses to stand instead. He has not surrendered, even though the Boer War is over. He sees the Treaty of Vereeniging as meaningless, and considers that document a heresy. The Boers have been betrayed. He's the feudal lord, and the self-styled governor of this barren province.

He issues an order.

"You are dismissed."

Petrus Nel bans me from the location. He's the lawmaker and forbids me to teach. His face is granite-like and forbidding. I turn away, and see, instead, the snow massed upon the Lootsberg like a treasure of pearls and diamonds. I reply.

"I disagree. I will go on teaching."

"You are dismissed."

"You fail to understand. This is a revolutionary age, and the ruling classes are finished. You can't ignore the Bolshevik Revolution. The Boers will not survive. The Coloureds and Blacks will inherit Africa and history will prove me correct."

"We are not Europeans. We fought wars in order to protect our land. We believe that God made the races separate. The Coloureds are our servants, and we are their just masters. There's no dishonesty. This is our traditional way of life, so don't even try and change things. You won't succeed."

His rigidity makes me despair. I will not leave New Kimberly, and no Brahmin Boer will give me orders. I side with the dorp's Untouchables.

"Meneer, I'm staying on in New Kimberly."

"You are dismissed."

"I accept that."

"You still insist on staying?"

"Yes. There is work to be done."

"You are foolish. Your work is over."

Petrus Nel glares at me, and leaves. I watch the angry Boer stalk out of my house.

The light of civilization returns as I read a line of Homer, and contemplate an ode of Keats. I see the peaks of the Lootsberg rising up with a pristine purity. There are treasures there, those pearls and diamonds of the snow-clad peaks. The Untouchables are treasures too; they are the black pearls scattered across the Karoo.

o　　o　　o

The mountains are serene, and the land is precious. Those herds of springbok will continue to leap through my mind with their shining bodies and will shudder always in my memory. I see the *bywoners* work the soil, and the tobacco plants struggle for survival, as the sky opens like an amphitheater. The wind sweeps past, and brings the dust clouds.

Ebrahim bursts into the room. This visit is no surprise. He struggles, as speech wars with flesh, and gesticulates wildly. He is like someone who is caught up in a maelstrom. He confronts me, and asks a question.

"You will not be here?"

I endure a moment of anxiety. I accept that Ebrahim, a slender Coloured boy of eighteen, is my favorite pupil. I regret his angry outburst, and fear that his lithe body might collapse under the burden of resentment. I pause, and contemplate the sparse winter grass and the red-tinged horizon, and the distant floating clouds. Then, I face the flagrant power of his young manhood.

"It's true that I've been dismissed."

"I don't believe it."

"Nel really meant it, and his decision is final. I've got no recourse to any appeal. It's all over."

Ebrahim groans, and I agonize too. The present is difficult enough and time has not erased the past. I recall an Indian girl, and her head was thrown back in ecstasy. She had jet black hair, and a ruby pierced her nose, and she wore silver bracelets. Her eyes held the sapphire gaze of a proud peacock. I recognize Kali, the destroyer, and she is still present in my life. I recall Gandhi's patience even in adverse circumstances. Ebrahim speaks in a bewildered voice.

"What are we to do?"

"Things just haven't worked out. The dorp supports Nel, and I have no friends here."

"Then we are both outcasts."

"Don't say that."

"It's true. I'm a Coloured, and you are English-speaking. We don't belong with the Volk. The Boers deny me my place in society, and they treat you with contempt. We are outcasts in the Karoo. I don't understand your surprise."

I admit that Ebrahim is right. Untouchables must remain as invisible servants, and a woman is always a dutiful wife. Yet I know that my association with Gandhi and support of the struggle is the real reason for my dismissal.

Ebrahim slumps into a chair. I've taught him for five years, and I think of him like a son. His features are delicate, like those of an Italian boy, and he has a dark mass of unruly curls. He's an intelligent and sensitive student. He's also a charming companion. He again speaks in a disconsolate voice.

"You will not be here. I just can't believe it. It's like a bad dream."

I must not indulge him. He must find his own strength and I reply firmly.

"You must still write the exam. It's only three months away, and then you will be free. You can make your own choices, and won't need me any more. My work will be over."

He is withdrawn, and his expression is introverted. Darkness falls and the comforting shapes of trees and even the koppies are suddenly obliterated. Yet, this darkness does not cloud his inner eye, and he sees other lands with lakes and mountains and their own blue skies. I light a lamp, and then he speaks with a poet's sensibilities.

"I do have a future, and it's got nothing to do with writing an exam. I'm taking on a challenge. I'm going to climb the Lootsberg, and I'll leap from the summit, and fly like a man-bird. I'll beat my arms like wings and keep on going until I reach Europe. One leap into that crystal air. That's all . . ."

"What will you do there? . . ."

He holds the mystery of the poet within. He is like a man before the fall of Adam and many visions rise in him like rainbows. He still has intimations of paradise, where things are yet unnamed. Love might then be called something else, and death is still to be discovered, while hope is an eternal burning bush. The future is all that needs to be understood. He will carve out poems from another universe. Africa explodes in his mind and it's a place of madness and death. Everything burns here and things are chopped to pieces. The Boers possess their own mandibles, and they masticate and belch. They are the new barbarians, who only add further to Africa's darkness.

Ebrahim speaks in a quiet voice. "I'll write poetry and forget about pain and uncertainty. Things will be different in Europe. The lake will be peaceful and the nightingales will sing in the forests. I'll live in a chalet and have a good life in Italy, or Switzerland . . ."

"It's not that easy . . ."

". . . I know that."

Cries of lamenting cattle sound in the distance. The animals struggle to survive and drought is their complaint. Other sounds and images echo in Ebrahim's mind, that have little to do with the Karoo. Romantic images of youth possess him. He sees the marble walls of old palaces, and hears the pounding hoofs of horses. He imagines that he picks ripening persimmons and red pomegranates, and tastes fresh bread, and drinks wine. He sees himself as a stranger to Europe. I take his hand and feel that fast pulse of excitement, and notice his flushed face and insist.

"You must fight back. You've got to stay on at school. Nel will appoint another teacher, and you will still be able to write the exam. You are no longer a boy. You are a man and should take responsibility for your life."

His expression is confused. I see that the child's dream of paradise is suddenly lost, and he's already a man who suffers. Still, he manages to speak.

"Fight? I don't know how. I can only think of ways of escape. I talk of climbing the Lootsberg, but even that's no use. I would fall out of the sky, and land on my parents' roof. I'd be disgusted by my mother's tears and my father's scolding. I know only one thing, that I'm being destroyed here. I hate this place. Even the river has given up. The riverbed is so dry, the water has ceased to flow. We are mirrored there. We Coloureds have forgotten how to hate. The Boers treat us like cattle, and we are just one of their herds. Our race is worthless, and we are just bastards. I can't take it any longer."

The lamplight flickers and casts its own shadows upon the walls. Troy rises and falls there, and lovers embrace and unite while ships are dashed upon inhospitable coastlines. Then, the winter snow ravages castles, and distant minarets sparkle in the sun. The darkness ebbs, and we struggle to reach one another.

"Please, I do understand. You don't have to say it . . ."

"I do possess a dream . . ."

"We all do . . ."

"Mine is different . . ."

"Is it?"

"Oh yes. I believe that I came here as a white child, from some foreign land. My blood is pure, and not tainted, like one of those Kaffir hordes. I was shipwrecked on the coast of Africa, and thrown ashore. Huge waves cast me upon a beach. The brown people found the casket, and took that beautiful white child and reared me as one of their own. I'm not a Coloured, I'm still that white child. My dream is intact."

He deludes himself. He's no imitation white. He is a Coloured, and belongs in the Karoo, and this dun land informs him. He is no survivor of a shipwreck. He's tenacious as the goats that crop the thorn bushes. He's clever like the jackal, and dangerous as the night adder. The rest is veneer. He's invented a make-believe life, and none of it is real. It's all romantic sentiment. I answer bluntly.

"You are not a white child."

Sweat runs down his cheekbones, and his eyes redden like a bull ready for a fight. His mouth tightens like a gladiator, as he pleads with a terrifying insistence.

"Don't you see? I'm not one of them. I refuse to be anything else. I'm not a Coloured . . . I'm not one of them . . . a hot-not . . . a boesman . . . a Kaffir. I'm white . . . white . . . WHITE. I'm an Italian boy . . . A Roman . . . A Parisian. I'm not a Capie, and I'm not a brown bastard either. I won't accept a hot-not bitch as my mother. I am that shipwrecked child. Don't argue with me. You only make matters worse. Just accept my story, that's all I want."

He lives out a terrible deception, and I must remind him about the facts of his birthright. He must not ignore the truth.

"There's no place else to go. The Karoo is your home. You are a Coloured, and belong here. We live in revolutionary times. The Great War has just ended, and we are not isolated from that event. I've read the newspapers, and shared in those reports from the front. I know about those tanks, senseless machines that churned up men and worms alike. I know about the poison gas that spilled into the trenches, and ate away men's flesh. Europe is devastated. We are better off in Africa, where there are new beginnings. Socialism is a rallying cry, and the serfs have risen in Russia. Gandhi preaches the doctrine of *ahimsa*, and we are not separate from these challenges."

He's shaken by a childish passion. He's not yet a man, and rages like an unmanageable adolescent.

"I don't care. None of this concerns me. I'm only interested in my own happiness."

"You are a Coloured, and this is your world. You should care."

"Shit. You mock me."

"It's the truth."

"You understand nothing. Sail off to Europe, and go and live in your castle. It's all yours, the heritage of a white skin. I want it too, and it's going to be mine as well. I am that shipwrecked white child. I won't stay here. I hate the Karoo, and I'll kill myself if I have to remain here. Don't forget that, because you are responsible."

"Stop it! This is senseless talk, and it's rubbish too, just like your nonsensical dreams. Neither of us is going anywhere. We'll stay and fight the Boers together. I'll coach you for that exam, and you'll better yourself. You'll find a job, a shop in Graaff-Reinet, where you'll tie up parcels and add up bills, and count yourself lucky. You belong to the working class. We all do. There are no more aristocrats left."

He stifles a sob, and flees my presence. He returns to the camouflage of the location, and will vanish there like an Untouchable. He digs himself in, and throbs and rages there. He's ticking away inside himself, a time-bomb ready to explode in 1920. He's made for revolution.

o   o   o

The Lootsberg mountains, with the dense clumps of bush, and weatherbeaten rock, tower. Forms cavort in stone: Hanuman, the monkey god, who is adept at scholarship, and makes sense out of confusion. Then, the wise *naga* serpents uncoil their subtle wisdom. They see through *maya*, and recognize the world as a clever illusion. Past and present are almost interchangeable, and there's only a flow of persistent images. The mind creates its own pain and happiness. The Indian Ocean flows. Gandhi's *ashram* appears. The Sabarmati river is close. Ahmedabad is on the horizon, and the city glowers. The sacred cows file past. There's a grove of pipal trees, and they give their shade. Gandhi approaches. He's spruce and wears a white *dhoti* and his eyes are smiling. He carries a staff, the trident of Shiva, and holds a child's hand. She's the Untouchable girl, and he's going to educate her. She's become his adopted daughter. Kasturbai follows him, and wisdom informs her eyes. The small procession moves on. The Untouchable girl dances, and Kasturbai claps her hands, while Gandhi leads the way. They climb the Lootsberg. The *naga* serpents throw down a ladder, and Hanuman the monkey god provides a map. Then, they reach the summit, that crystal heart of mountain. Gandhi rings that anvil there. The mountain sings and the sound is awe-inspiring. Suddenly, the dark continent is purged. The land behind me is like a sea, and the light across the foothills is white. We talk on the verandah. The afternoon allows a respite of warmth. My host, Abraham de Loor, speaks.

"How do you like 'Bergzicht'?"

He's an enthusiastic amateur farmer. His lined face and stooping body of a former judge from the Transvaal settle uneasily here, like a tree, withstanding the drought.

"It's a beautiful place."

"We are close to the mountain."

The Lootsberg towers, and attempts a seduction of the sky. They cut us down to size, and we are like flies on the face of the earth. Abraham de Loor speaks again.

"Hard soil . . . poor crops . . . and always drought. This is our heritage, so we survive because of the silence and the sight of the mountains. Do you understand that it's enough for me?"

The old man pauses, and shuts tired rheumy eyes. Yet images from his life remain there; faces of men and women: the criminals, the liars, the deceivers and the innocent. The perpetual conflict between the state and the individual still wars within him. It's not surprising that the land has become his balm. The Lootsberg wipes out the contradictions within his soul, and the many miscarriages of justice which he witnessed fall away. He needs the sight of mountains. I answer.

"Yes, I do."

Abraham de Loor opens those tired eyes, and he's become the watchful hawk. He guesses the reason for my visit, as I turn away, and avoid his probing look. I contemplate a dense clump of trees, and admire the fat merino sheep, and note a small dam that holds precious water. I sense that the rocks merge with the silence as the air vibrates and nothing moves. The Lootsberg is an ivory mountain, with a crystal center. Gandhi informs this heart of rock. I can no longer avoid speaking and must now answer Abraham de Loor's questioning look.

"It's those others, the men of this dorp, who use me as a scapegoat. They resent my presence here, and denounce me as a radical. I am a woman, and I want a man's power. I've chosen my own course in life and I won't be deflected now just because angry men criticize me. I want to know the culprits. Give me their names . . ."

Abraham de Loor is reticent, and a gulf opens between us. The thicket of trees is suddenly tinged with a golden light. The veld holds myriads of secrets. There are meanings now under stones, and the thunder has a voice, and the sky is a face, while the castor oil bush holds wine. A monkey swings from a tree. I see only Hanuman, the monkey god, and the sand is his subtle calligraphy. The *naga* serpents uncoil their hidden meanings here. I believe that there is a code that can unlock the universe. Then the Indian Ocean will flow here, and Sabarmati will be close, and the sacred cows will be able to wander freely, while the pipal trees will give of their shade. Gandhi will spin the *khadi* cloth, and Kasturbai will stir the pots, and then liberation will come even to the Karoo.

"Don't magnify things."

"I'm not."

"There is talk. This bitterness after the Boer War still festers here, even though the war ended twenty years ago. Then, we've been through a drought, and a poor harvest. Nobody is happy."

"It's more than that."

Abraham de Loor flushes, and pushes a dottle of tobacco into a pipe and grits his teeth on the stem. He speaks, and adds his own disapproval to the Boers' condemnation of me.

"It's this Coloured boy."

I see his prejudice take shape as a foul worm that wriggles in front of us on the verandah floor.

"Is that all?"

"It's enough, Christina. Get rid of this boy, and make an end to gossip. This slander is unpleasant."

Abraham de Loor sides with the Boers, and is prepared to support evil laws despite his high calling as a judge.

"Sexual innuendo . . ."

"I didn't say that."

"I don't care. I'm teaching Ebrahim, and he will write the exam."

"You are making a mistake."

"I won't be bullied. Petrus Nel doesn't intimidate me. I've taken my decision. There is no going back, and I won't even reconsider it."

I think of Gandhi. He takes the hand of an Untouchable daughter. I stretch out toward a son, Ebrahim. We will travel together across the droughtlands, and escape the Boers and their jackal faces. We'll reach the Lootsberg mountains, and there will be no celestial ladder for us to climb. Instead, we'll need rope and an ice axe, and crampons. But we'll make it, despite a harsh ascent. I affirm this intention now, for I am still that *satyagrahi*, a passive resister involved in Gandhi's struggle here. I hear that crystal gong sound in me.

"This is foolhardy."

"I'm doing what's right."

"Let's not be moral."

"I am."

"You are a determined woman, but this is going too far. Nobody wants a fight. This is a Karoo dorp, and the Boers will not accept racial equality. Don't try and force anything. This is not the liberal Cape. Why are you surprised?"

"I believe that people must change, and then revolution will happen here, even in this remote Karoo dorp. Petrus Nel, even though he behaves like a feudal lord, will not push the clock back. This is the twentieth century, and socialism is the driving force. The Boers must recognize this, otherwise they will fail, and that would be a tragedy."

"You are a radical."

"Why do they hate me?"

"There is no conspiracy."

"This dorp censures me, and you can't deny that. I know that I am a threat, and the Boers are against even me. I can smell their hatred. It's a male sweat like the stench of an animal, and I've known it before. I first encountered it when I experienced a baton charge during a protest meeting which Gandhi led in Johannesburg. We tried to storm the Asiatic Office. I remember that it was a windy day. The Mounted Police rode in, and they were arrogant men on horseback. They reflected the barbarism of our time. They were the new Goths and Vandals already charging. They wielded their batons, but they might as well have held clubs, or spears, or stones. They struck out not for survival but conquest, and they battered and brutalized innocent women and children. They raped us of our dignity, and intention to do good. Now you see why I fight. It's this ignorance and darkness in men's minds. It's the confusion of barbarians, Stone Age creatures, henchmen of darkness."

Abraham de Loor witnesses my struggle, and I feel like someone who is drowning. Even the veld has darkened, and a murkiness tarnishes trees, and stones, and sets dark clouds in the sky. Prejudice pollutes everything, and only the rain can wash it away. This is the rain that ends a drought: Gandhi's rain-like tears of compassion.

"Christina, you exaggerate. The Boers are upset, but they are still decent men. They are country people and they lack the sophistication of town folk. They are also out of touch with the rest of the world. They forget that even Cape Town and Johannesburg exist, let alone London and Europe. You must take all this into account. You are the one who is prejudiced."

"Who is the villain?"

"Nobody. It's the general opinion. The Coloured must go back to the location. That's all that's required, and then the dorp will be satisfied."

"I don't accept that. This is the Boer War legacy. It's a mistrust of the English, and a fear of Kaffir attack. All this is still very much alive here. Yet specific individuals are responsible. What about Wim Pieterse?"

"Nonsense. Wim Pieterse is no gossip. He's an upstanding man, a successful wool merchant. No, definitely not Wim Pieterse. You are mistaken."

I agree that Wim Pieterse is an upstanding man. Yet I remember those cold blue eyes, and that avarice for land. Wim Pieterse is not entirely innocent, and he would like to see me leave New Kimberly. I throw out another name.

"What about Piet Barnard?"

Abraham de Loor smiles with real pleasure and enjoys telling me about Piet Barnard's good fortune.

"Piet's in love, but it's not a woman, this time. No, it's a horse, a proud Arab stallion. Piet is a rich man, and above reproach."

Last week, Piet Barnard galloped past on that fine Arab stallion, and I sensed his veiled hostility then. Yet I will not argue, and just call out another name.

"What about Jan Volschenk?"

Abraham de Loor treats this suggestion as a joke. He replies with suppressed mirth.

"Christina, don't defame the butcher. I know that he's a formidable man, and intimidates everyone. But he's no executioner in the dorp. He's just the butcher, a man who knows his job. His mutton is excellent and he doesn't overcharge even you. He's on the side of his customers. This is your worst mistake. Give it all up. There's no point in specifics."

He teases me now, and I'm not easily humored when dealing with matters of principle. I know that the butcher is part of this conspiracy of silence, so I try another name.

"What about Kobus le Grange?"

"That's unthinkable. Le Grange is the auctioneer, and he wouldn't make such a mistake. He values his clientele, and even you, Christina. You might buy another house here, or a stinkwood kist, or fine linen. He needs your business too, and you are also a customer. He's too clever to slander anyone, so he's not your man."

Abraham de Loor defeats me. He implies that these Boers are innocent of careless talk. I don't believe him, so I probe further, with another name.

"Frans du Plessis?"

"The locksmith?"

"A peeping Tom."

"What have you to hide?"

"My good name is being questioned . . ."

"Christina, this is ridiculous."

"I wish I didn't feel betrayed. I can't believe that the men of this dorp are against me . . ."

"You exaggerate. The Boers are upset, and that's natural. But they are all decent men, and nobody dislikes you. That's a foolish idea."

"I know, but I'm still angry. What about Charl Myburg? He's a fine Greek scholar. He knows the classics, and is familiar with Aristotle and Plato. I don't believe that he's narrow-minded."

"He's certainly no liberal . . ."

I think instead of Andres Perreira who is of Portuguese ancestry. The vision of Vasco da Gama must inform him, and I sense his questing intellect, and roving spirit. The epic voyages of discovery still thrill him. The map of Africa must surely be traced in his brain. He's not dwarfed by the Lootsberg, or trapped in these droughtlands. He's not one of these petty Boers. He's a European.

"What about Andres Perreira?"

"Don't make a mistake here. Andres Perreira is a Boer too. He's become one of us, and given up any claim to his European heritage. He's settled here, and works his lands. He won't support you, Christina."

"Someone is guilty."

"Be careful."

"I've mentioned names, and you deny everything. I agree that trouble is brewing in this dorp, but I won't stand by and see Ebrahim sacrificed. I won't become the scapegoat either. I'm not responsible for troubled times. The Boer War! The drought! This has got nothing to do with me. I have only one more suggestion. Willem Goosen might be the culprit . . ."

"You are wrong about Goosen. He's a strange man, and I can understand your suspicions. Nobody can fathom him. He talks to his sheep, and lives apart from the dorp. He's got little to say. But he's not guilty. Give up this game. I've heard gossip, and the talk is general. Listen to me now. Send this boy away, and let him go back to the location. He's a laborer, and not a scholar. We have no place for 'Coloured' gentlemen. You make his life difficult, and he'll suffer because of you."

Abraham de Loor reflects ugly prejudice. Discrimination is like a disease. The whole dorp is infected. I answer.

"It's the moral question. I am teaching the boy, and it's my duty, and also what's right. Neither the Boers, nor the state, will make me think otherwise. Petrus Nel rules this dark province, and you've allowed lawlessness to take over. You are responsible. I pity your weakness, and must forgive you, because of your age."

"Christina, this is an insult. You do not sit in judgment. I've been on the bench, and I know about judging others. One struggles to find humility first, and then one tries to see with God's eyes. It's not a human affair, but an attempt at divine wisdom. You shock me."

"Men insist on a divine mold. Women are different and they must speak for themselves. They carry so many burdens. The many unborn children of generations. The failed ambitions of their mothers. The frustrated and angry rebellion of so many sisters. They cannot afford to speak for God. They leave this onerous task to men, who do it much better. After all, God is a man."

A foul pit opens here, and the stench of it is terrible. It's like the contagion of a plague. This racism will spread as a dark and polluting cloud, which blows across the land, and threatens all.

Even the Lootsberg mountains appear tarnished. This contamination is worse than the mustard clouds of the war, that noxious poisonous gas which spilled out into the trenches. I simply know that I must disobey. I no longer even question Petrus Nel. He is just a warlord, a ruler of a dark province. I move out into open revolt. I will take Ebrahim's hand for he is my Untouchable son, and we will begin our trek, and move across the droughtlands. We'll have our sight of the crystal mountain, and the gong will sound for us. I embrace Gandhi's vision of Africa. The task is the ascent of a mountain, a journey toward equality.

o   o   o

I reflect upon Ebrahim, and his tumultuous imaginings; he is a knight of history; a heraldic messenger of kings; a poet of splendor. He fills me with longing too, and I believe that he will make this journey. He'll cross the droughtlands, and elude the jackal-faced Boers. He'll outwit them. He's one with the eagle, and runs like an antelope. He's a king cobra. He'll climb the Lootsberg, and ring that crystal gong. Ebrahim turns toward me, with a dark and brooding face, and insists:

"You don't really know me . . ."

I have no doubt as regards his identity for he is Ebrahim, my Italian boy, with those stunning good looks. He's my gifted pupil from the location, and he's also a Coloured of this Karoo. I answer honestly.

"You are Ebrahim."

"That's no longer my name. I am someone else."

"I see. What's your real name?"

"Alphonse . . . or Charles . . . or Edward . . . or Christopher . . ."

"I prefer Ebrahim. Try and accept your birthright. The Karoo is your home. It's a good place in the world, and it's a good deal better than many others. Africa is no longer isolated. We are linked to other nations, and move out of this dark age. The revolution is very close."

"I don't care. It's got nothing to do with me."

"It has and you are affected. Gandhi worked here and he had a dream of a classless society. We are all part of his vision, and no one can insist on their own private dream any longer. We've got to work together."

"I refuse . . ."

"You are being stupid."

"I am myself, a shipwrecked child, a foundling washed up on the coast of Africa. I'm not one of them. I'm not a brown bastard, and I don't come from a hot-not bitch. I'm white like you, Miss Ransome."

"Take care . . ."

"Listen to me. I am the son of a noble family. I'll pursue my own dream, and nobody can take it away from me. Not even you, Miss Ransome."

"That's enough! You seem to have forgotten that there's been a Great War, and that Europe is devastated. The snow falls there now, and it covers the dead, like a white shroud. Those shimmering lakes brim with tears, and the nightingales are silent. Nobody can afford your dream because it's simply not available anymore. The nineteenth century is over. Romantic notions no longer hold. Even the forests have become battlefields. There's nothing left."

I've deliberately tried to dispel his fantasy. Now, he writhes and makes excuses.

"I can't help it. I need my own dream, otherwise I'd go mad."

"I don't think so."

"You don't understand."

"I think I do. I understand quite clearly that you insist on 'your own dream.' But I'm talking about reality. I don't deny that shipwrecks occur, and that there are victims. I have met other castaways, who survived an authentic disaster . . ."

"Politics again . . ."

"You listen to me now . . ."

"All right . . ."

"I'm talking about those Indian immigrants, the first indentured laborers who came to Natal from Madras. They were the true castaways thrown up on the coast of Africa . . ."

I am reminded of Sanjay Pillay's family. He, as a small child, with his father Raj, and his mother, Devi, were castaways here. They were thrown up on the coast of Natal and suffered hunger and deprivation and also injustice. Sanjay was the foundling; my lover was this child of shipwreck. But Ebrahim is different, a Coloured born in the Karoo, and he can adapt, take root here, and survive. Ebrahim is no weakling. Sanjay was an offspring of Indian culture, a man confused by the caste system, and part of a feudal era. He saw wealth as a necessary acquisition. Women were only possessions, and religion combined both sex and power. Ebrahim has not inherited this culture of India. He is simply part of Africa, a seed of vitality, and he need only recognize his destiny. The revolution is taking place now. The Karoo is his bunker, and he must ride out the chaos. He'll survive among the Stone Age Boers, and outstrip them into the twenty-first century. I believe that a golden age is at hand. I continue speaking to Ebrahim.

"I had friends among those Indian castaways, Sanjay Pillay, his father Raj, and his mother, Devi. They left Madras and Raj recalled seeing the Chepauk Palace turn red on the horizon. India receded, and Africa reared up in their imagination. They reached Natal, after a long and arduous voyage, but they found no better life there. They had been duped by unscrupulous recruiting agents, and were just another form of cheap labor. Raj cut the sugar cane, and Devi gathered it up. They lived out in the open without a latrine or washing facilities, and food was always short. Raj constructed a hut out of branches and leaves. They knew that animals in the Indian jungles were better off. Raj became bitter, and Devi contracted tuberculosis. My friend Sanjay was confused, and truly suffered a shipwreck."

Ebrahim is interested. He senses a real story, rather than a lesson.

He asks:

"What happened next?"

"The castaways were rescued. Gandhi reversed their fortunes and salvaged that shipwreck. He piloted those survivors to less troubled waters. He transformed these desperate men and sad women, and made them revolutionaries. They were the first passive resisters, and they brought the idea of *ahimsa* not only to Africa, but also to the world."

"I've heard enough . . ."

"All right."

Gandhi's voice reverberates in me, and echoes here between Ebrahim and myself. I stand again on the Natal beach, and Gandhi speaks out of the ocean, and its waves. There's a sound of swarming bees. I see the palm trees, and the sugar cane is another green sea. The sun is a mirror of brightness. I walk across warm sand, and Kasturbai joins me. She is barefoot and glows, in an orange sari. Her bracelets jangle with a musical sound. Her skin is dark as sandalwood, while her face is wrinkled and old. She reflects all India. Many women reside within her; the goddess, the obedient wife, the fertile woman, the holy mother, the barren hag. She struggles with these submerged identities. She follows after Gandhi, and his tracks are lost in a desert. She sees him vanish on the horizon. She simply needs to be herself. She makes a soundless cry. She has a hunger for life. I understand. Ebrahim scowls, and is impatient. I only know that I must continue talking about Gandhi, and those Indian immigrants.

"We must consider Gandhi. He was a seasoned campaigner, and also a stretcher-bearer during the Boer War. He nursed the victims of bubonic plague, without regard for his own safety. That happened later in Johannesburg, after the war. He'd come to terms with himself, and contemplated death serenely. An oriental dispassion informed him always. He was a man who could discipline an army and also tame men with strong and difficult natures. He taught greedy men about generosity, and made angry men peaceful. Gandhi was an impressive leader, an honest politician, and a saintly man. He still is. He works in India now."

Ebrahim is restless, and I refuse to yield to his boredom. I wonder if I've spoken truthfully for I revere Gandhi as my own teacher, and inspiration. Yet, there are contradictions in his nature. The marriage of this "holy" man and his "obedient" wife is an enigma. Their strained relationship disturbed me. The scalpel of my intellect cannot separate truth from idle speculation, and there's no solving it. I continue:

"Remember, the fight isn't just about politics, but also the human condition. There are problems of race, and of caste, and women need a voice too. We must not forget evolution. We cannot ignore revolution."

I think of the sesame seed, and it symbolizes the power of *ahimsa*, as well as the strength of hoes and spades. The sesame seed contains Gandhi's universe. I hold it in my palm and Ebrahim cannot ignore my gesture for I offer peace. He takes my hand, and I feel the nervous grip of an adolescent. The sesame seed—Gandhi's vision—is lost. I've failed to reach him, and anger claims him instead, as he speaks out of his own inner chaos.

"I go back to the location each evening, and it's as if I'd switched out a light. Civilization ends at your door. Things outside are fearful. I glance over my shoulder and see the Boers shake their fists. Women stare from windows while their snarling dogs bark at my heels. The walk home is scary. Then, I enter a candle-lit room, and shadows leap out from the walls, those ancestral figures of the Kaffir wars, and Moselikatse again charges the white settlers. Anguish surges within me. There are clashes in my nature, and battles rage within. My family thinks me mad. My mother weeps, and my father is confused, and my brothers curse me. I need my own dream. I am that shipwrecked child."

"Take care . . ."

I cannot say more. Anger confuses him. He cannot escape this land. The Karoo is inside him, and the images are already branded across his eyeballs. Springbok leap through the burning hoop of his mind. The Lootsberg is a serene cathedral of stone. This is an interior vision, and one that can never be obliterated. I speak again.

"Take care. It's not easy. Try and accept this birthright. You might not find another place. A refugee can have nowhere else to go."

He refuses to believe me. He denies this vision, and curses that birthright. I want to weep at this display of ignorance. He answers.

"What are you talking about? There's no beauty there. The thorn trees are ugly, and the drought disfigures everything. There's just the gray veld . . . and the gray sky . . . and the gray stones . . . and the gray people. I want some other place, and I'll find it. I believe that."

"Think again. This is your birthright."

"Shit! It's not mine. I won't accept it. I'll kill myself if I have to stay here. I'll hang myself from a thorn tree, or drown myself in the mud of the riverbed, and struggle there like an eel until I suffocate. I'm not staying."

"You fool."

"I don't care. I'm leaving, and I'll get the hell out of here. I'll find another mountain, and it doesn't have to be the Lootsberg. There's the Alps, and the Himalayas, and the Andes, and these other mountains can delight me. I'll find a lake too because I'm tired of drought, and dried-up rivers. Those nightingales will sing for me. I'll become that Italian boy who lives on Lake Geneva, or Como, and I'll find that new world. That's all I want, the right to enjoy my life."

"I'd like to agree with you, but it's not possible. The recent war has devastated Europe, and the war clouds have not yet lifted. I believe that civilization founders . . ."

He is suddenly a lost, small boy, and turns a wan face toward me, as he asks:

"Where can we go? What can we do?"

I pause. His face is a brilliant candle in a dark world. I too possess my own dream. I again walk across that beach in Natal, and the sand is soft underfoot. Gandhi meditates upon a rock. The Hindu scriptures tell of the immortal sage, who takes to the skies in the form of a swan. He is one such immortal. Gandhi's aspirations soar, as the wind takes up his message, and the waves are a crescendo, and the pebbles echo his cry too—a shout of REVOLUTION. Then, the white beach is suddenly empty, and I stand alone. The immortal swan flies on. Gandhi found only a resting place at Phoenix, and bestowed his gift, the sesame seed, which crystalizes the power of *ahimsa*. The might of passive resistance, and the cry of REVOLUTION fills me too. I am a true *satyagaihi*, and I shall reshape my world. I share this dream with Ebrahim, as I speak again.

"There is a place, Gandhi's *ashram* in Natal, and it's a bastion against the oncoming dark age. You would love it there, and I'd show you the distant sugar cane fields. The *ashram* nestles beneath green hills. We'd sit on straw mats, and listen to Gandhi, while Kasturbai serves the tea. You'd feel so contented, and at peace. Then, we'd march outside, and take on the planting. I'd give you a spade, while I'd manage with a hoe. You'd find this experience of honest work a renewal. I wish I could take you there. I haven't been back since Gandhi left for India."

Ebrahim is both interested and curious. He senses how my past resonates at Phoenix, and insists on learning more. He asks: "Were you alone at Phoenix?"

He puts pressure on me. The mountain obscures my view. The white beach is washed away. The holy man is absent. The great swan flies on. Gandhi has returned to India and presides at Sabarmati. Factories belch their filth there, and the industrial city of Ahmedabad pollutes the air. The river flows nearby, and the sacred cows wade. Gandhi cares for the Untouchable girl, and she is his beauty now. He treasures India's filth, and carries away the nightsoil. He is the true alchemist who transmutes shit, and makes dreams out of turds. Kasturbai empties the chamber pots. She's made me heir to her sorrows, and I accept this burden. I am her rebellious daughter, and I'm fulfilling her task of disciplining men, and liberating women. She's taught me, and now I've become her tool. I speak with her sharp tongue, and I know how to stab. I've learned how to sew up wounds, and I know the feel of flesh. I understand her vision of the world, for she is a renounced spirit, a woman's body that moves within the intense activity of life itself. I live even though, as with her, love has died and I find it hard to revive it again. I'm forced to think of Sanjay, as I answer Ebrahim.

"Yes, I had a friend."

"Who was he?"

Ebrahim is persistent, and I know that he would approve of Sanjay. My Indian lover possessed his own blend of Romanticism, so Ebrahim would surely recognize a comrade. I answer.

"An Indian. I've already mentioned him: his name was Sanjay Pillay. He came here as a child and was an Indian immigrant, one of those indentured laborers of Natal. He was damaged by the experience of shipwreck. He turned to Gandhi, not really looking for a philosophy, but for survival in this country. He was a Brahmin, an Indian aristocrat, who behaved like a prince, and believed that his caste gave him that privilege. Nobody cares here, for we have our own racial problems. So Sanjay suffered throughout his life from being misunderstood."

"Tell me about Sanjay."

That relationship had many different aspects. The images of a maharaja's pink palace walls crowd me, and these shadows of India illuminate my mind. I recognize Sanjay as a handsome and tragic man who was shipwrecked on the coast of Africa. He saw himself as a Brahmin king who lived in a summer palace in Kashmir, within sight of snow-capped mountains. He dreamed of drinking glasses of cool sherbet and possessing the women of his harem. He could not survive in Natal. Our relationship was doomed, for we were a mismatched couple, a Brahmin and a revolutionary woman.

Ebrahim is interested in my past. He's like an archaeologist in search of trophies, and interested in Sanjay's restoration.

"Tell me more."

"He died."

"You were left a widow?"

"We weren't married."

I resent this cross-examination. I feel agitated when I think of Sanjay, who was the embodiment of a powerful energy, and a distiller of love potions, and a maker of amulets. He possessed and delighted in that sexual energy which Gandhi sought to sublimate. Both men represent the polarities of Indian religious experience, the sensual Tantricist and the renounced yogi.

"No. I wasn't married. I'm not a widow. I lived out an experience of sharing with another person, and I learned about my own survival. It's not an easy subject to talk about."

"You don't sound happy about that love."

"There were complications."

"The man loved someone else?"

"Not exactly."

"What, then?"

"Sanjay believed he was a Brahmin, and insisted on a caste superiority. He never embraced *ahimsa*, or fully accepted Gandhi's teachings. The passive resister and the Brahmin clashed, and there was no easy resolution, for scripture and tradition dominate an Indian man. They yoke a woman into subjugation. I know that Sanjay had a child-bride. This love affair of mine is like an oriental text, reflecting a lack of wisdom, betrayal, and impenetrable customs. There, I've told you everything . . ."

Ebrahim is astonished, and gapes at me in amazement. I need to keep him as my ally, and he must condemn this barbaric custom. Child marriage is an insult, not only to me, but to all women. He fumbles, and then asks, bewildered:

"Is that being married?"

"Yes. It's an Indian marriage, a valid contract for Indian men, and the legalized abuse of female children. A brutal and one-sided form of marriage. I can understand your confusion, as it's a heinous custom."

"Did you ever meet her?"

I pause, for even I find difficulty in grasping the strange elements of Lakshmi's personality. She still influences my life, and I see her almost as a dark force, often a presence more than a real person. I answer:

"Yes, I did encounter Lakshmi."

"Tell me about her . . ."

"She was like a river, an eternal girl, an Indian girl of fourteen with an incandescent glow. She wore strings of silver necklaces over a red and gold sari, and a ruby was displayed in her nose. Her breasts undulated beneath the sari, while her belly rippled slightly. Her face was an open lotus. She was stunning in her power to hold, and even destroy, a man. She was like an aspect of Kali, trampling her consort in anger. She reclined among fine silks. A tapestry of Hanuman, the monkey god, decorated a wall. Burning candles illuminated an effigy of Shiva, and cakes and fruit were offered there too. She was a woman ready for copulation. A Tantric goddess."

"You went there alone?"

"I found a pretext. It was easy, as she didn't know me. Sanjay had never spoken of me. He had no need to. She was so secure in her harem, and I was no threat. Incense burned in the room, and a bowl of sweets lay at her elbow, while a small white dog crouched at her feet. She offered me a sweet, and it had a sickly taste. I had such an odd sense of it all. The girl appeared totally passive, and immature, and would remain so. She was a cave, into which a man vanished. Her voice would always be unheard, and her conscience would remain dormant. The problems of society would always be unknown to her. She was simply a concubine. Yet her existence forced me to question my life. I'd chosen independence, and fought for my freedom. I did not think I'd lost anything, but the image of Lakshmi left me bewildered. I did what I thought was necessary. I insisted that

Sanjay give me a child, and fell pregnant. But it all went wrong, for I had a miscarriage, and then Sanjay died. I saw things end. There are no rules for happiness."

This memory exhausts me now. I have made my choices. I've never married, and choose to be childless. Yet none of this is sufficient. This love affair is not a tragedy, but more like a comedy of errors. I've forgotten too that I've been confiding in a young and impressionable boy, and my past surely presents him with a new and bizarre set of questions. I certainly have not meant to influence him. He whispers, with an unexpected ardor:

"What about Lakshmi?"

"I don't know. She's dedicated to the art of copulation, as much as those female figures on temple walls, who intertwine with males, or other females, or a bull, or a goat, or an elephant, or a *garuda* bird, or even a bear. She's so much part of Indian life that I can only visualize her as the breast, or thighs, or mouth of some consort in the embrace of a many-headed one hundred-armed deity."

"Please. Don't be anxious. There's nothing wrong. It's just that I already know all this. I've seen these images in my dreams, and it's the hidden language of my flesh. I too could love a child-bride, and she will be like those images on Indian temple walls."

Ebrahim's words stun me. His answer is a betrayal. I observe him with Kasturbai's grave eyes, and I am burdened with her sorrow, and must keep this pain and doubt to myself. I have unwittingly placed him in the role of Sanjay. I have revealed the power of the phallus. The imperviousness of a Kaffir chief lurks in his eyes. We are out in unknown territory now. The Lootsberg mountains rear up like an *impi* of darkness that will fall upon this dorp in an act of destruction.

o   o   o

A day of brilliance, as the winter sunlight spills, and preserves the Karoo with a crystal clarity. The Lootsberg mountains rise up, and appear but a hair's breadth away. Abraham de Loor is my visitor. His gnarled hands are at rest. He observes me shrewdly, and speaks.

"Spring will be here soon. Then, the trees will turn and I'll be glad to see the end of winter. The drought needs to be broken."

"Yes, I'll be glad to see the spring . . . and the rain."

"I'm certain your fig tree will bear fruit this year."

"I hope so, but I think it's barren."

This exchange of small talk is futile, and it helps neither of us solve the problem of Ebrahim. He's a restless student possessed by his own adolescent dreams, and now he thinks only of Lakshmi, the goddess of temple walls. We are both trapped in the same Indian dream. Abraham de Loor senses my distress.

"This place gets you down?"

"The dorp irritates me."

"Is that all?"

"It's enough."

Abraham de Loor stretches with difficulty, a necessary painful maneuver, involving stiff knees and joints. He's an old man, and I should be more sympathetic, yet I confess to resenting his interference, as he probes again.

"You are worried."

"Please . . ."

"I'm not intruding. It's just that I care, so don't be embarrassed, or even angry. That's not my intention. I only want to help."

I am reticent because I know that Abraham de Loor disapproves of Ebrahim. He's like the other Boers, and supports New Kimberly, and the dorp's public censure.

"It's not just Ebrahim. It's other things too . . ."

"Don't live in the past . . ."

"It isn't easy . . ."

"You need to be more positive . . ."

"I'm trying. Give me a chance."

Abraham de Loor is like a remote father. He is a decent man, and an attentive listener, and I do need to talk not only about Ebrahim, but also Sanjay. The two men fuse in my consciousness. The proud and arrogant Indian prince, and the desperate and selfish Italian boy, have much in common. They form a single painful dilemma in my life. I try and share this problem with Abraham de Loor.

"It's many things . . . Ebrahim . . . Sanjay Pillay . . . Gandhi's return to India . . . my own loss of purpose . . . I wither here in the Karoo."

"I'm not surprised. You need to talk."

I pause a moment. I need to free myself of my own image as a strong and independent woman. I understand now, for the first time, the impact of my visit to Lakshmi. Her situation told me that I too was fragile, and in many ways a fugitive. I too needed to be adored. This insight shatters me now. I remember that I took an oath with one man, Gandhi, who demanded that I too extinguish my ego, and serve others, with a detached sense of love and self-denial. I had also given myself to Sanjay Pillay in hungry abandonment, and insisted on fidelity in return. These commitments remain now like debts that I have conveniently forgotten, and must now repay. I speak.

"I feel like some kind of a victim. In India, there are solutions for every occasion, ritual forms of behavior that appease guilt. I can even understand those Indian women, who, when they are widowed, commit *suttee*. Life has ended for them, and there is no man to serve, so they throw themselves upon their husband's funeral pyre. There's even some sense to it. It's an expiation, and so guilt ends. There's no future to bother about while love remains consummated, and the fire is the final marriage bed. I know the difficulty in living after a loved one has died. I experienced that pain after Sanjay's death. My own life is still meaningless . . ."

The intricacies of my thoughts are like conundrums, and they are labyrinths opening out inside me. Yet my words do not put

Abraham de Loor off the scent. He refuses to feel sorry for me, and doesn't scold either. He remains an impartial listener, who uses his voice sparingly. His eyes ask the questions instead, and they are the mirrors of all men. The questions reflected there are cruel, and I should demand a woman as my judge. He speaks.

"Go on. We are not looking for any solution. You must just make an end to suffering. Even guilt wears itself out, and it's not like a chain that bites into the skin, but more like a stain. You wash that stain over, and over again, and it doesn't go away at once, but fades a little more each time. Then, one day, when you look for it, the stain is gone. It will be like that. The pain won't go away immediately, but it will begin to diminish, and then disappear."

I listen to Abraham de Loor's advice, and wonder if he's correct. I've been here so long, as a prisoner, under the white-faced mountain, that I can hardly imagine being elsewhere other than within sight of the Lootsberg. I answer.

"I suppose there was a conflict right from the beginning . . ."

"Only you know that."

"Yes. Gandhi, on the one hand, called for purity and renunciation. I really believed in him. He had such peace and inner resourcefulness, yet he often talked of how he had originally been a man with a violent nature. Somehow, he had tamed the demon inside himself, and it never escaped again. His nature remained pure. But, despite being in touch with Gandhi's spirituality, and trying to embody that ego-less quality in myself, I still surrendered to the deceptive charm and sexuality of Sanjay Pillay. Neither of them claimed me in the end. Gandhi returned to India. Sanjay died, and the love affair was a failure."

"What do you mean?"

"Sanjay's upbringing. He came with his parents from India. His father was a jeweller from Bangalore, and his mother came from Mysore. Those are Indian cities of such splendor, with their minarets and towers and temples that hold the mystery of the *lingam*. There are cults that worship Shiva. The variety of life is so enormous there. Sanjay's father, Raj Pillay, made a pilgrimage. He journeyed to the Ganges. He saw the river fall in torrents over rocks, and the eagles and vultures circled overhead, as corpses collapsed into the waters, and the pyres burned everywhere. The banks of the Ganges were crowded with pilgrims, who wore their brilliantly-colored garments, and bells tinkled and priests chanted prayers. The pipal trees grew close by, and Raj Pillay found a quiet spot where he offered the sacred thread of the Brahmins to this holy river. Then he traveled to Africa. Years later, deprived and destitute, he ate with low-caste men in Durban. He'd broken his caste, and never recovered. Don't you see, Durban was worse than any monsoon. Sanjay could never survive such a past . . ."

"I agree. You took on too much in loving this man."

"I tried. We lived together in Natal. He was the perfect Brahmin, a member of that high caste, and wore the red caste mark branded on his forehead. He behaved like an Indian prince, even though his background was humble. He refused even to think about how his parents came here as indentured laborers. I tried to be like an Indian woman, but I wasn't happy surrounded by Indian brasses, those fierce and benevolent gods, with their hundreds of arms, and protruding tongues, and the fierce mothers of death, trampling their consorts, and brandishing swords. All those hungry gods of procreation, who were in union with the universe, stifled me, and robbed me of my sense of myself. My sari was more like a shroud, and it always reminded me of *suttee*. Yet, I fought back, because I am not a passive concubine. I am an emancipated woman."

I pause and ponder upon Sanjay. The river of love throws up its own shadows, those images of passionate love, and these memories intermingle with dreams. I believe that Sanjay has been reincarnated, and prowls the dense Punjabi jungles as a tiger. He may even rule a kingdom as a powerful nawab, and could even reside in that summer palace in Kashmir. He was a man split between East and West, a distiller of love potions, and a maker of amulets. He played at being a Brahmin king. He never accepted Gandhi, and rejected the virtuous doctrine of *ahimsa*. He was inwardly violent, and uncontrollable as his inner conflicts warred within him. He insisted on his child-bride, Lakshmi, the goddess of temple walls. She anoints the *lingam*, and applies the *ghee*. Her face is enigmatic. The copulation of the gods. The cloying air of India. The heavy scent of temples. Mother India spawns her offspring, Sanjay and Lakshmi. They are her divine children, the *lingam* and the *yoni*. I confide in Abraham de Loor.

"Sanjay took a child-bride."

"That's immoral."

"It's true,"

"He slept with her."

"Yes."

"I'm shocked."

Abraham de Loor is out of his depth here. So was I, when it all happened to me. I remember those days when I fought Lakshmi even in my dreams. I recognized her seductive and manipulative powers. India impinges on Africa, as Asia's complexity clashes with that darkness. Battles are lost and won. The Kaffir wars still echo, and the Boer War just goes on, with the Mausers still firing, and the assegais do their damage too. India moves in *kalpas*; vast aeons of time, where empires rise and fall, and decay sets in, and hunger and thirst and sex go on. That's the perpetual cycle of India.

"It's gone on for centuries, this hateful custom of child marriage. Rajas and their concubines and men consorting with children. It's just an endless act of copulation. That's the Indian way of life. It's not just the population, for every temple wall boasts its images. The gods copulate too, and they intertwine with bulls, or bears, or elephants, or serpents, or *garuda* birds. Sex is a religion of its own. India's image is one of procreation. There's no escaping it."

"What can I say? This man abused you. You must have found such a relationship unendurable . . ."

"Please, Braam, we are dealing with India, and customs that are strange to us impinge on every aspect of life there. The different races are divided into castes, and the Brahmin has all, and the Untouchable possesses nothing. It's not so surprising that Sanjay had a child-bride; even Gandhi was no different. He too married when both he and Kasturbai were only children . . ."

"It all seems so barbaric . . ."

"This is South Africa, and we are far away from India. Yet I was forced to get used to this arrangement. Sanjay defended his child-bride. Her name was Lakshmi and she reclined on a pillow with her head thrown back. Her breasts swelled beneath a red and gold sari, and her hips were rounded too, while tinkling bells ornamented her ankles. She wore strings of silver necklaces, and her mouth was like a rose, and there was a ruby set in her nose. Her olive-skinned body was lithe and supple, as she moved her slender arms. She was ready for the act of copulation: I recognized that as soon as I saw her. I challenged Sanjay, and informed him that this custom was rotten and deceitful. He disagreed, and insisted on visiting his child-bride. I countered that slavery was once an acceptable custom, even though now we abhor that form of degradation. Child marriage is no different."

"I find this man's behavior monstrous. I've seen ugly situations in court, but this surpasses everything. Christina, I had no idea of the enormity of your suffering. I'll do everything in my power to help you."

"Sanjay was clever. He reminded me that Gandhi had taken a child-bride, and it was true. I respected the marriage between Gandhi and Kasturbai. They had married when they were children of thirteen, and played out their 'game of love' in Gandhi's father's house at Porbandar. Later, Gandhi was consumed with guilt, and thought only of his own spirituality and virtuous conduct. Then he became an attorney in Durban, where Kasturbai mothered his sons. There was a crisis, and she suffered an internal hemorrhage, and bled from the uterus. He saw her sapped and drained of energy. She underwent an operation and harsh instruments probed her womb, in a kind of surgical rape. He meditated upon the fact that 'she was no longer a temptress.' She was used up, an exhausted old woman at the age of thirty. He took a vow of celibacy, and made her the mother of an *ashram*. Kasturbai is terribly connected to Lakshmi, as she belongs to an older generation of child-brides. They are both abused, and I am vulnerable too . . ."

Abraham de Loor expresses bewilderment and even finds my words a little embarrassing. He shrugs and says:

"Why do you torment yourself?"

I smile and recognize that men have blundered through my life. It's not just Sanjay with his abuse, although he was certainly the most overt and unconcerned. It's the others, too, like Gandhi, with his promise of liberation, and Ebrahim with his needs and desperations. He betrays me now. He misses lessons, and insists on being alone. I know he's not kicking a stone, or playing hopscotch in the dust. He's not bird-watching in the veld, or doing any press-ups at home. He only dreams about making love. I know that he adores Lakshmi, and imagines himself as her lover. He's drugged with incense, and has lost his reason. I answer Abraham de Loor. The hidden meaning is revealed.

"All women are Lakshmi. They are Kasturbai too. They represent youth, and age. The full cycle of a woman's life. The menstrual flow becoming one with the ocean. Then, the walk across sand, with a vision of the temple in the sky. It's simply the meaning of life and death. That's all."

o   o   o

Snow is a white clasp on the Lootsberg. The mountain possesses its own mysteries. It's not only Gandhi who rings that crystal gong. Other secrets hide there too. There's a Bushman painting of a woman who dances eternally in a beaded skirt. She contains her echoes too, for the life of the Bushman is frozen in this ecstatic dance. There are handprints of warriors who have left their mark. Their identification in time lives on as the conqueror's fist. That remains too. Bushman, Hottentot and Matabele roamed this land as uncrowned kings. The petrified and frozen images remain too, some fossil shells swept up here by an ancient sea during the time when the Karoo was only an ocean. Prehistory groaned and swelled here, as reptiles were magnified and the plant life threw out its own sure tentacles. Then, volcanic dust covered all. The Lootsberg holds this history, and it's an inner chamber. Time's receptacle of useless bric-à-brac, a hidden soul.

Ebrahim is a recalcitrant, and a restless student. He scowls, and pushes back a lock of unruly hair, as he complains:

"The dorp never lets up . . ."

"What do you mean?"

"There's always trouble."

"Tell me."

"It's become so familiar, the same old story of abuse. Faces staring at the window. The butcher shook his fist, and the auctioneer swore at me. Two other men made lewd remarks. People set their dogs on me. I can't take their shit, and I've got to get out of here."

His words are upsetting, and he makes even me feel ashamed. I can't believe that burly Jan Volschenk would threaten a boy, and Kobus le Grange, the auctioneer, is a sensible man. Yet he humiliated Ebrahim. Others among the community made lewd remarks. I don't understand it. I can only blame the drought, and it's taken its toll among us. The Boers also let dark thoughts fester, and it's as if a gangrene infects them. They find things intolerable, and they react with words or actions that amputate. They are capable of anything; the Boer War proved that. The British won, yet the Boers are the survivors. Ebrahim's position is vulnerable here. The Boers must leave him alone. He has a right to dignity. I answer:

"I'm sorry. Things are ugly in this dorp, and I've no right to even question your desperations. I can only say one thing, and that's that you must write the exam. Then, you are free. You'll be able to get a job, and leave New Kimberly."

He gives me a wan smile, and I notice that tired lines show about his eyes. He answers with a trembling mouth.

"I'll try."

We both know that the dorp is not the only problem. He is concealing something, and his face is clouded. He's on his own. He shares nothing, and we've become strangers. Still, his face is a map, and I can read the direction there. I sense that he's in love but I cannot guess at the woman's identity. The Boer girls are away at school, and none would be interested in a Coloured. No girl from the location would satisfy him either. He has these Romantic ideals, and needs to worship a goddess. He's still devoted to an idealized Lakshmi. There are no child-brides in New Kimberly, yet's he's found some temptress, and she's here in this dorp. The wonder lurks in his eyes, and a man's experience flashes there, with the magical knowledge of another's flesh. It's the golden hue of his irises, and he's suddenly grown up.

The problem is that this Coloured boy mirrors Sanjay. He's unaware of my suspicions, and that I'm baffled and in a turmoil. He reties his cravat, and combs those unruly curls. He preens before a mirror. I've changed too. Kasturbai's face looks back, the mother of the *ashram*, with her disciplined civility and austere gaze. Ebrahim's polite too, and calls out a reassurance.

"I won't be long. I'm taking a walk out in the veld, and I'll take my history book and memorize some dates. That will help. I do want to pass the exam."

"Yes. The air will do you good. Don't be late: there is work still to be done. The Napoleonic Wars, and Pythagoras' theorem."

My voice sounds hollow, and I am like Kasturbai when she instructed the ashramites. She doled out plates of food, and handed out hoes and spades. She was formal and polite, a mother who did her duty. She hid her shame and masked her pain. She feigned a wise detachment, and was her own shield against sorrow. She was adept at private mourning. These are ridiculous thoughts. Kasturbai was a good and excellent woman, and I'm trying hard to be decent too. There's nothing wrong with either of us. Yet I cannot banish my own desperations that go deeper than Kasturbai's stoical presence. It's got to do with Sanjay's part in my life, and Lakshmi's influence. This dangerous past ramifies here in New Kimberly, and I must not allow that history to be re-enacted. There must be an end to disaster. I rush out into the streets of New Kimberly, and will search out Ebrahim. He must not surrender to a woman. There is too much of my own life at stake, and I'm forced to cry out:

"Ebrahim! Ebrahim!"

He's vanished, and out of sight. He's had a good start, and it won't be easy to find him. These shuttered houses hold their secrets. The lives of the Boers are top secret, classified information. I can guess at their unlisted possessions; a kist of fine linen, a stack of Mauser rifles, a precious family Bible, a purse of gold sovereigns. There are other secrets too. Those private dossiers that deal with confidential case histories: family feuds, brother against brother; deep racial hatreds, the loathing of the British, and the fear of Kaffirs; infidelities, the deceived and grieving wives; bankruptcies and frauds; the sinners who have lost their faith, and no longer believe in God; the endless struggle with drought. It's all happening here in New Kimberly. The dorp is a microcosm of the world.

I look toward the mountain, and the jagged Lootsberg pierce me. The dark peaks rise up, and obscure my future. Gandhi's vision is crystal clear, the idea of a new society, even in South Africa. He must blow that conch shell, and again rouse me to a sense of my own pristine awareness. Then I won't be lost in these droughtlands, and New Kimberly can no longer claim me. I'll take the hand of my Untouchable son, and we'll cross the mountains, and reach the outside world, and reclaim our history. We'll camp in the Uffizi Gallery, and dance with the statuary of Greece, and sail on Shelley's immortal lake. We'll dream together, and defeat this dusty land. We'll put this remote dorp behind us.

Wim Pieterse interrupts my thoughts, as he points to the Lootsberg in admiration, and comments:

"Juffrou, it's a rare sight. The Lootsberg are so clear."

"They look like the Alps. Snow crowns the summit."

"Cold nights still. The temperature plummets below zero."

"I'm looking for the Coloured boy . . ."

Wim Pieterse expectorates stale tobacco juice. He's no longer that refined and lanky Dutchman, but just another bigoted Boer. He's as contemptuous as Petrus Nel. He's marred my view of the Lootsberg so that now I see only the jagged peaks of an unassailable fortress. The Lootsberg isolate New Kimberly, and cut the dorp off, so that no news reaches people here. They've heard nothing about the Great War, or the Bolshevik Revolution. Gandhi's cry goes unheard in this arid place. I only know that the Boers are intransigent, and Petrus Nel is determined to push the clock back.

A horseman approaches, and I recognize Piet Barnard, who sits proudly on his new Arab stallion. He pauses, and nods in brief recognition. I say:

"That's a fine horse."

"Ja, Juffrou. It's an Arab stallion, a beauty even here in this dorp where we have fine horses and good cattle. I'm proud of this stallion."

"Did you see a Coloured boy?"

Piet Barnard recoils, as his restless hands tug at the reins. He sees me as a traitor to white society, and he's no longer polite, but only shakes his head angrily, and rides on. I ignore this slight and recognize these men as cowards. They choose to regard me as a radical. I don't maintain the traditional way of life, and fight for revolutionary change, and passive resistance is still my weapon, so I refuse to give in to anger and prejudice. Ebrahim must trust me, and write the exam. He mustn't fool around with a girl. That would be a disaster. I'll leave then and ford the drift, and travel the road of dust and hardship, and reach Graaff-Reinet. The walls of this dorp won't hold me, and the poplars will not blind me with their beauty, and the sky will give me back my freedom. I'll escape the shadow of the Lootsberg. I'll forget about the Boers, and leave New Kimberly.

A man herding a flock of sheep approaches and Willem Goosen runs with his own kind. He barely notices me, and no greeting is exchanged between us. He whistles to his sheep, who nod and respond. He runs barefoot, and his face is sharp, with bright eyes. He's a strange child of the Karoo, rather like a Hottentot. His white skin saves him here. A Coloured could herd those sheep. He carries a knife and kills for the pot, and lives off the veld. He sleeps out in the open and has no proper home. He skins a goat and collects wild honey, and has the ways of a Hottentot. He's not a real Boer, but some aberrant creature.

I arrive at the trading store, and the Boers are out in full force. A cattle sale has just ended, and I overhear snatches of their conversation. ". . . Those merinos fetched high prices . . ." comments Kobus le Grange, while Basie Viviers chimes in, " . . . I thought those Afrikaner cattle splendid animals." Jan Volschenk, the butcher, adds: "Many fine carcasses too." Piet Burger takes a pinch of snuff, and insists: "Cattle feed, that's the problem." The Boers suddenly notice my presence among them, and they are immediately silent. These middle-aged men show their disapproval of me. Only Ben Potgieter raises his hat, and I walk away, and leave them to their business.

I refuse to be intimidated, and can't even be bothered with them. The Boers can think ill of me. My own life has its priorities now. The serene Lootsberg rise up with a pristine purity, and their beauty makes all else inconsequential. I will no longer be imprisoned in these droughtlands. Those jackal-faced Boers don't scare me. The hawk flies as a sentinel here. I've a glimpse of Gandhi's vision, and recovered my own integrity. Petrus Nel is no longer an enemy, and the Boers are my future friends. Ebrahim will write the exam, and then my work will be done.

I'm almost prepared to call New Kimberly home when I reach

the door of the de Bruyn house. Ebrahim emerges from that Boer home. It's as if a vision of the sea throws him up at my feet. The sunlight strikes his face, and it's a weapon of circular power and brightness. His intrigue has been revealed. He has been with a woman.

PART TWO

The Seduction

Ebrahim turns a tormented face toward me. Petrus Nel glowers, and his eyes pierce me, as if he will disfigure me with his anger. The Lootsberg rise up, like a dragon uncoiling its power, and these peaks mirror Nel's wrath. The Boer points an accusing finger at Ebrahim, and shouts: "RAPE."

This accusation makes me stagger with pain. Ebrahim wrestles with handcuffs, and dark bruises show on his face, and he's also had a nose bleed. This is an unlikely and ugly charge, and I dispute the matter.

"Lies! I don't believe it. I know Ebrahim, and he's like my own son. He's not capable of rape. I just don't believe you, Mr. Nel."

"An offense took place."

"It's not true."

"I'm afraid it is."

"Who is this girl?"

"She cannot speak."

"More lies."

"It's true. This Hottentot raped a simple-minded child, the daughter of Pieter de Bruyn. There is no doubt. The Coloured is guilty."

Petrus Nel delivers his blow. My mind reels as I inwardly repeat the accusation . . . an offense took place . . . a white girl was raped . . . Pieter de Bruyn's simple-minded daughter. The anguished face of Ebrahim offers no clues. He's just a baited animal who cringes and whines. He's surly and obscene, and Nel has corrupted him. The Boer turns everything to filth.

My house is tawdry now, and nothing shines or gleams anymore. Even my books withhold their knowledge. My flesh crawls and I want to vomit. I sense the wind rising up off the veld. We here in the Karoo are scorched under a sky of steel and pushed to the end of our endurance. I can't endure anymore. I must examine the facts. An offense took place . . . a white girl was raped . . . Pieter de Bruyn's simple-minded daughter . . . Ebrahim is guilty. I begin to understand. Ebrahim did come out of the de Bruyn house, and I sensed that he had been with a woman. More distant connections appear, too. Lakshmi! She is here, the eternal girl, who flows like a river, that most perfect of all children. She wears strings of necklaces, and her sari is red and gold. Her face is like an open lotus. She is Kali, the destroyer, and she will use her power. She burns like a flame, and we are all her victims.

Ebrahim's face is dark and angry, and his eyes tell me nothing. I speak, and request a favor of Nel.

"Please, I don't refute this charge. The gravity of the situation appals me. I ask a favor, Meneer. Don't refuse me. You will lose nothing by this kindness. The facts are bewildering, and I want to talk to Ebrahim alone. Please allow this."

Petrus Nel struggles with my request, like a man already seduced by his own sense of power. He sees himself as a feudal lord, and now craves a general's authority. He rules this remote region, and his kingdom is New Kimberly. He answers:

"Fifteen minutes! Don't ask more of me. I want the Hottentot here when I get back. I want him alive. I don't want to shoot down this jackal, so he must not try and escape. You are responsible, Juffrou, and you must be careful. He's a dangerous man, a mad baboon who terrorizes the dorp. He's both ugly and evil, and we will make certain that he never rapes again. He'll go to jail for life."

Ebrahim is like a cautious animal, who fears a blow, or a kick, or a bullet. The boy understands the code of the bush. I watch Nel move off, and he momentarily scans the room, then lurches out. I turn to Ebrahim, and face the boy's anguish, as he blurts out:

"I didn't rape Sannie de Bruyn."

I believe in his innocence. I'm sure that he didn't rape the Boer girl, but I suspect that he seduced her. I also feel betrayed and cheated and angry and answer severely:

"Prove it."

Ebrahim turns on me, like an angry snarling dog. He wants to savage me now as well as the Boers.

"Miss Ransome, you betray me. I have only respect for you and gratitude, yet you condemn me like the others. You've joined the Boers, yet I don't even care. I've lost Sannie de Bruyn, and I loved her dearly. I accept my degradation and the fact that Nel spits on my life."

He sobs, and snot pours from his nose. He's in a wretched state and I force myself to speak in a kinder tone.

"I know. I know that there is some explanation. You must try and tell me, and then it will be easier. I've always helped you. I still believe in you."

He smiles, and I dab at his face with a handkerchief, and clean up those superficial cuts. He's appreciative, and touches my hand. I sense distant echoes in this situation. I recall when those mounted police charged and used their batons, and Kasturbai staunched wounds then. I do the same now, and emulate her compassion as it gently flows here, and experience the wisdom of her glancing eye. She is the mother in my breast, the one who can sustain Ebrahim. She is the wisdom treasure in my heart. Ebrahim speaks.

"Try and understand that Sannie and I are alike. We are both deprived. I come from the location, and I'm branded as a Coloured. She's a retarded white child. There were no barriers between us. She didn't see my skin color, and was not offended by me. She didn't call me a hot-not, or see me as a bastard. We were both outcasts."

"Tell me more."

"Adults don't understand, and I don't think you will either. The Boers call it rape, but it's just not true. We love one another. The Boers can punish me, I don't care. I'm not afraid of their prison. I've been there many times in my dreams. I only know that this love is my protection, and then I'm not afraid. The Boers won't defeat me."

He's defiant, and it's all useless: Petrus Nel will crush him. He's just a worm under the Boer heel, and they will trample upon him. They see him only as a jackal, and they will shoot first, and then kick over his body. The Boers will spit on his carcass. He doesn't stand a chance.

"The Boers are clever. You've outraged them, and they'll never rest. You are the victim, and love won't save you. You must tell me everything, and then we'll seek legal advice. There will be a charge, and you must be defended."

Ebrahim flounders as he wrestles with the truth. He will have to tear it from his own breast, and encounter all the hidden lusts and vanities of his nature. He finally speaks.

"It was a game. I was the Italian boy, and she was a Voortrekker girl. She had a toy wagon, and two black dolls, and clay oxen. We traveled in the wagon, and forded swiftly-flowing rivers. We made fires at night in order to keep the game away. We heard the lions roar, and the elephants charge close by. Yet, we were always safe. I held Sannie in my arms and she laughed and kissed me, and I responded. Then, the game got more exciting when the Kaffir dolls charged us. They were an *impi* now, and these warriors came down from the koppies, and rushed out of the darkness. I felt so confused. I wanted to acknowledge my own dark blood. I felt the need for conquest, for I am one of Moselikatse's sons too. Yet, my white blood triumphed, for I was also that baby in the golden casket, who was washed up in a shipwreck. I am the Italian boy. I fought off the Kaffirs. I was like a brave Boer, and relied on my Mauser. We won the battle, and Sannie cried with relief. We slept close to the wagon, and she gave herself to me. Nothing mattered then, and we didn't care about her father, or even you, Miss Ransome. We'd found love, and that's what's important. The Boers won't destroy us."

"I see . . ."

The moment is stale, and I feel flat and deflated. I sense only the power of Lakshmi moving here. She is the influence now. Her jangling bracelets rattle even louder. Her nipples are erect like tiny sea shells, and her thighs are parted. She flows between us like a river and carries us into dangerous waters. I force myself to speak.

"You seduced her . . ."

"What do you mean?"

"The girl is fourteen. She's under age, and she's also simple-minded. You committed a crime, and that was a stupid mistake. It was also very wrong. You are guilty of an ugly and ruthless seduction. You deliberately took advantage of a child."

His mood turns angry as he draws himself up. He does suggest a pagan power, and he's severe as any of Moselikatse's warriors. He's right in believing that their dark and angry blood flows within his veins too. He snarls, and raises a fist, and the manacles shine like bracelets.

"It isn't true. I'm talking about love, and you know nothing about it. You are an ignorant spinster. You've given up, and yet you dare to judge me."

He insults me and I can no longer control my own anger. I reply bitterly.

"I made a mistake in trying to help you; you aren't worth the effort. You are a despicable seducer and you abuse women. Petrus Nel can deal with you. I don't care anymore."

Ebrahim sobs, and we both regret this acrimony. I long to soothe his distress. His physical beauty assaults me. His eyes are lustrous, and his face is a classic profile. The bruises are only superficial. He is my Italian boy, with a slender body, and cast in Sanjay's image, with taut thighs, a tongue that is a swimming fish, dark butterfly lashes, and the olive skin of a Mediterranean man. I allow this desire to pass. He has cohabited with a child, and Sannie has kissed those lips. She has caressed him, and feasted on his body. I want no part of his splendor. Instead, I view him with Kasturbai's grave eyes, and resurrect the boy from the body of the man. I see only an injured and abused child, and whisper softly.

"All is forgiven. There must be no harsh words between us. I'll arrange for your defense."

He smiles and presses kisses on my hand, and the bond between us is re-established. He responds to Kasturbai's firm hands, and my own disciplined voice. I'll get over this "other woman": the Boer girl and Lakshmi are just names for infidelities, and mean nothing other than my own failure in love. We are like a mother and son. I grasp the hand of this Untouchable child. We'll cross the droughtlands and evade the jackal Boers.

Nel appears at the door, and fills the darkness. He brings with him all the uproar of the dorp. He embodies the righteous and just anger of the Boers, who are on the side of truth; God is their judge. They see us as the decadent elements of a dying civilization. We are the Leftists, the defeated revolutionaries, the radicals. Our rage will leave nothing intact, and we will tear down every established institution. Revolution is close to anarchy, and neither God, nor government, nor the bourgeoisie will survive. Nel suspects our treachery. He's the jackbooted tyrant here, and his will is like a grenade. He'll even blow us all up, before we succeed and turn him in. Yet he's the law here and must maintain the status quo. He instructs the police sergeant who accompanies him, and apprehends Ebrahim.

"Time is up, and the truce is over. This ugly business must be dealt with by the courts. There is a docket, and the charge is rape. This Coloured is under arrest. The sergeant will take him into custody."

Ebrahim does not resist, and accompanies the sergeant. He is just a stripling, an innocent young life, a brutalized victim. The process of the law begins and this rape charge will have its repercussions. I flinch inwardly. Gandhi's teachings don't help. This is dealing with filth, and the accusation spreads like a stain. We are all tainted. Ebrahim is led away, and I call out a reassurance:

"Have courage. We are in this together, and I will not desert you."

Nel remains even after Ebrahim has been taken away and is aware of my distress. For we are being battered in stormy seas about Africa's inhospitable coastline. We both know that white society founders and Ebrahim will be the only survivor in the twenty-first century. I speak:

"This charge is false. Ebrahim did not rape Sannie de Bruyn. He loved the girl, even though she is under-age and retarded. It's not easy to understand this relationship. The boy is only guilty of a seduction, and there are extenuating circumstances. He is not guilty of rape."

Petrus Nel's lips curl in a sardonic sneer. His energy is fierce as a furnace, and he insists on chalking up his own moral code.

"I call it rape. An outrage took place. There is no mixing of the different races in South Africa, and Boer and Coloured must live apart. This is our traditional way of life. We are not a coolie nation, and we tolerate no miscegenation. The Coloured is guilty."

"You are deluded. There was no rape and Ebrahim is not guilty."

Petrus Nel is unrelenting. He possesses an inflexible will and refuses to budge an inch. He demands Ebrahim's soul, and he's convinced of his own purifying vision. The might of Jehovah works through him, for he is an Afrikaner and a Calvinist. He speaks:

"The Hottentot took the child. It was done against her will. She is afflicted, a simple-minded child, otherwise she'd have fought for her virtue. She'd have been a tiger, and torn this rapist to pieces. Sannie would have died for her virginity. The Coloureds are tainted by the sin of the Europeans, because our ancestors took their women in lust. We suffer now because the Coloureds remind us of our weakness. Our European blood works against us, and we too suffer evil temptation. The races must be segregated, and it cannot be otherwise. You take the Hottentot's side. The rape doesn't upset you though you are a woman and have delicate feelings. You should be upset and weeping like the Boer women. Instead, you choose to insult me . . ."

These contemptuous words don't defile me. I struggle to maintain my own calm. I recall Sanjay Pillay and our days together. We were sitting on that Natal beach, and the sea was close, and the sand was a white spell. The ocean was another kind of purification, with the froth of the sea like semen. We did not make love that day but rather allowed the spilling sea to wash us, and the pebbles under our naked feet to remind us of the earth and its power to sustain. The banana trees shone behind us, and their flat green leaves held a promise. I touched a pomegranate and we shared its fruit. The sugar cane fields were distant. I listened to the voice of Sanjay as he read from a Hindu epic, and knew peace that day, interpreting it as the light of the sun and the wash of the sea. I choose to squander this memory now and share it with Petrus Nel. Gandhi would approve of this sedition.

"I don't find Ebrahim's encounter strange. He loved the Boer girl, and I understand. It's quite clear to me, for I loved an Indian."

Nel recoils as if I'd struck him in the face. He's like a wounded man who bleeds internally. He's morally stunned and unable to recover easily. Still he manages to denounce me.

"You are a sinful woman. You and the Hottentot are agitators. You try and undermine society, and corrupt others. I won't stay in the same room with you. I leave you to your sinful ways. The Hottentot will be punished. There is no saving you either."

Nel's eyes dart about. He's furious now, and his paranoia is loosed, as he checks his tongue and holds back his abuse of me. I can imagine that he would like to call me a bitch, a whore, a strumpet, a tart, a radical, a kaffir-boetie, a revolutionary woman. He lurches out of my house like a man suffering from a gunshot wound. He will be back. I sit with my head in my hands, and examine my own feelings. My emotions are turbulent. Love tears me apart, and Ebrahim torments me, and Sanjay haunts me. There's that resemblance between them, for they both possess the seductive quality of brown men. I recall Sanjay's lithe dark body, and Ebrahim's supple good looks. I don't believe it's just a matter of sex. This feeling also embraces Gandhi's dream of a classless society. Nel feels threatened, and the Boers attempt to secure their laager. They won't succeed. I've torn an opening there. The black shadows spill in, and Moselikatse's warriors will walk openly in New Kimberly.

o   o   o

Ebrahim roars through my dreams. He is the young lion now, with claws extended, ready to trample upon the honor of the Boers. I wake to find the events of the night before a burden. I recall Petrus Nel's intractable will and explosive anger, and know that he will take his revenge with the suddenness of a plague of locusts falling on fertile land. Then, we will be in ruins. I'm consumed by restlessness, and I ache with a dangerous and insatiable curiosity. I must see the Boer girl. Lakshmi is somehow involved in this intrigue. The Indian girl who is incandescent, and like a rainbow shining. The eternal girl who is like a river. Kali works her power here, and the Boer girl and Ebrahim are her subjects.

The Boers ostracize me. Anger and resentment clash behind closed doors. Women in black dresses ignore me. The Lootsberg rise up and the mountains are indifferent to the cry of rape. My neighbors reject me. Jan Volschenk closed the door of his shop in my face, and Piet Burger only grudgingly served me in the trading store. Frans du Plessis and Kobus le Grange both made disparaging remarks, and I distinctly overhear the words "Hottentot" and "bastard." Charl Myburg tipped his hat in greeting, but the effort was noticeable. Willem Goosen stared at me from behind a tree. Andres Perreira blabbered a greeting, and his words were incoherent. Ben Potgieter and Basie Viviers discussed a "trial," and they did not lower their voices when I passed by. Piet Barnard's face is like a thundercloud, and he refuses to acknowledge me. Petrus Nel watches, and bides his time. He has an appetite for strife and discontent. He will choose his moment and then attack.

I take up my stand outside the Boer girl's house. I know the wait will be long and I am prepared for any delay. My hunger for this vision is powerful. Her perfume seems to fill the air like the cloying incense that smoldered in Lakshmi's room. I cannot separate the two children. The shadows outside dance like a retinue. I'm certain that when I enter the Boer child's room, she will be surrounded by those deities of Indian temple walls, and I will not be deceived again. I know the infamy of these immortal children.

I retreat into the shadows. Shapes like those of Ganesh, the elephant god, Hanuman, the monkey god, the *garuda* birds and *naga* serpents appear to fill the trees. I imagine that they will soon step down from those temple walls and dance here in ecstasy. Then, without warning, the de Bruyn family file past and walk in the direction of the Calvinist church. I move out into the late afternoon sunlight with a clear head. I move stealthily into the house. There is no guard. There is no need of one, for Ebrahim is behind bars. The house of the scene of the rape is thrown open, so the dorp can come and smell and taste the taint of this coupling. But the bed sheets are not hung up as curtains, and the Boer child is not dressed in black like her elders. The Mauser rifle does not rest close to the bed, and the warning cry of "Kaffir! Kaffir!" remains unsounded. A swarm of bees flies past. I push open a solid and heavy oak door, and enter the Boer girl's room.

Sunlight blinds me for a moment. The brass bedstead gleams with an authority of many afternoons of love. There is a familiarity here. It is not Lakshmi but Ebrahim who pervades the atmosphere. He is a sultan and Sannie is his princess, as she lies propped up in bed. There is no Indian paraphernalia and the angry-visaged deities do not invade here. There is no rising incense or the cloying scent of an oiled and seductive body. Yet a confusion still reigns in the room of the Boer child as I note the scattered cushions, toys, sweets, children's books, toy building blocks, a family Bible, a small accordion, a riding crop, a lace collar, a white kappie, dresses, sprigs of veld flowers, and the already familiar clay oxen, toy wagon, and black dolls. The Boer child and the Indian girl are both careless children and abandoned women.

Sannie smiles and displays fine teeth. Her mouth is a crimson cupid's bow that is seen more often in Renaissance painting than on the faces of Boer children. She is like someone who has just woken from a dream. A princess, who has slept for a hundred years, is embodied in her form. I half believe that she will wake and recover her lost intelligence, and then she will be animated by a wit and precocity far beyond her fourteen years. I recognize that youthful sexuality which stirs in those full breasts and wide hips. Sannie examines me too, and no doubt notices my tired and red eyes, and that my hair is awry and that the sweat of yesterday's terror still clings to me. She makes no conversation but offers me a sweet. I bite into a sticky toffee and regret it. Ebrahim's spirit is still locked up in this room, for he is the master here, and she is his concubine. I was right about a retinue. The many-armed Shiva, Kali, the dark mother, Ganesh, the elephant god, Hanuman, the monkey god and the *garuda* birds and *naga* serpents do not cavort here. Instead other entities move in this room. Ebrahim has recreated those mirages on the horizon. Florence, at the foot of the Fiesole hills, and the river Arno flow here. He's introduced the statuary of the Uffizi Gallery, strewn here with the Karoo sun pouring in at the window. He's made a cheap reproduction of Italy for himself and the Boer girl. Naples on the Tyrrhenian Sea floats here, and objects from Herculaneum and Pompeii stand side by side with Karoo stone and calabash. Ebrahim is indeed the Italian boy, even in his conquest of the Boer girl.

The Boer girl suddenly dispels the mirages on the horizon, and demands her own authenticity. The immediate business of the day begins. She claps her hands and is a small mimic of adult authority. She is the woman in charge now. She crowds small toy figures into the wagon. I watch closely, for this is the game which Ebrahim described; I am about to witness a repeat performance. I fill in my own details, and watch the Voortrekker wagon move off into the interior. Kaffir *impis* wait in the hills. I keenly observe a battle, as the Boer girl moves the two black dolls in aggressive combat against the wagon. I also imagine those chubby hands caressing Ebrahim. Petrus Nel is not wrong, and makes no mistake in fearing a disaster. The threat to the Boers is real and the black invasion and retreat into the laager are ever-present realities. There is always a need to protect white women, and the dorp must view with grave concern this so-called rape. A black has penetrated the laager, and the community is no longer safe. Ebrahim must suffer the consequences. The purity of the white race is at stake. This will be no ordinary trial.

Sannie takes cherries from a bowl. She is indelicate and spits out the pips. A clumsy child replaces the seductress as she stretches out for more sweets and rifles the tin. I reflect now that the Boer girl is innocent, and has the honesty of Voortrekker women. She trusted the Italian boy. I wonder if she even misses Ebrahim. His part in her life may be no more significant than the black dolls and toy wagon. She just goes on playing the same game alone. She's no different to the dorp. The Boers are threatened now, and it's as if the Kaffir wars, like the Boer War, are never really over. A stray shot, a vendetta, any incident will trigger off these old wars. There's nothing new to fight about.

There's only the coldness in men's hearts and the blindness of their eyes. This is a seed of darkness, the slumbering death in us all.

o   o   o

There are footsteps outside, as frost cracks, and stones are dislodged. I half expect to see the demented figure of Ebrahim. The whirlwinds spin in the distance and the sun is a luminous disc, as the dust clouds whirl above the Karoo. The elements force us to endure and much is being tested. Little is being forged anew. These are the events before a revolution, when ordinary life falls into disorder, and moral anarchy prevails. Ebrahim does not triumph. He is not the first revolutionary across the barricades, and occupies no Boer installation. He is safe in jail.

I open the door and greet Abraham de Loor. His tired eyes search my face, as he anxiously takes my hand. His palms are icy. He speaks.

"Christina! I had to come . . ."

"You've heard the news?"

"Everyone is talking. A rape charge is a serious matter, and I find it unbelievable. This is New Kimberly, we are just a quiet dorp."

I shrug helplessly even though I'd like to offer comfort. He's an old man, yet I still cannot wipe out Ebrahim's folly. He must just accept things as they are. This rape allegation will have its consequences. I answer:

"Thank you for coming. There's little you can do, and I wish it were otherwise."

Abraham de Loor's wise eyes appraise me. He is visibly upset, as we all are. This community is rocked as if by an earthquake. Nobody is exempt, and everyone in New Kimberly is involved now. He speaks.

"A rape! It will be a long and bitter trial. Anger and aggression will be on display. There'll be mud-slinging and sexual shame.

That's the worst aspect, and then there'll be no acquittal. There's no comfort here."

I know that he's right, in that filth and ugliness will parade as morality. Ebrahim will be broken in spirit. A foul pit opens here and the stench is suffocating. I plead with Abraham de Loor for assistance.

"You must help me, Braam. I've got to defend this case. You must recommend legal counsel."

Abraham de Loor pauses. He's not in his dotage yet, and he once again demonstrates his resourcefulness. He speaks calmly.

"Don't worry, it's all arranged. I have spoken to an advocate."

"I'm grateful, but who is this man? I can't recall any liberal advocate in the district. Have you talked to someone at the Cape or even in Johannesburg?"

Abraham de Loor is still my kind and clever friend. He's not been defeated by bad turns, or gout, and he's different from the other Boers. He speaks.

"I took the liberty of speaking to Marius Greyling. He's from New Kimberly, but he's been abroad for many years. Now he's returned home. He attended Leyden University, and he's a liberal Afrikaner, almost a European. He's the man for this case. I expect him here this morning. Trust him with your confidence, and don't hold anything back."

I gasp with relief, and the day is not so hopeless. The wind that plays havoc, as it lifts the dust clouds off the veld, is unexpectedly tamed, and will drop at sunset. Then the Lootsberg will rise up as the serene guardians of the dorp. The vast hinterland will be bathed in a warm glow of light. I answer.

"This advocate must help us. Ebrahim is no faceless cipher, and more than just a boy from the location. He's a valuable member of a new society. I put only good things in his hands, I'm not to blame. The Boers defeated us. His adolescence became warped and his psyche was twisted. They are responsible, and the location is their creation. The Boers will pay a price; the guilt and the shame is theirs."

Abraham de Loor disagrees, and my words challenge him. He rises, and insists on defending the Boer cause. He is roused to drubbing up his own feelings for Afrikaner nationalism. His face is florid as he speaks.

"Don't blame the Boers. You are English-speaking and resentful. You turned to Gandhi, and his resistance campaign, and flirted with liberalism. We are not fooled by such ideas, because we know where we stand. We are Afrikaners and this is the Karoo. The Coloured must be punished. He raped a white girl, and there must be justice. The Boers will see to that."

"Braam! This is ridiculous. Why are you defending the Boers?"

"I'm an Afrikaner. Our war is never over. We lost the Boer War. Our tenure here is always uncertain, and we've got no place else to go. England is not our home, and neither is Holland. I live here, and I have a vision too. The ideal of a new kind of Afrikaner, an enlightened man in Africa. This has got nothing to do with British colonialism, or even Portuguese high adventure. It's a belief in the emergence of a 'Renaissance man' in Africa, a leap of fire in the heart. Poets and artists know this experience. It's the quest for an ultimate and searing beauty that is here even in Africa. We cannot return to Holland, because that country of Europe cannot hold us. When we trekked, we saw extraordinary sights: the vast mountain ranges, escarpments like inland seas, and rivers that watered all Africa. The Karoo is only one such marvelous place. We are men made big by these landscapes. We Afrikaners have rediscovered Africa. We have become like princes, rather than soldiers of fortune. We were suddenly soldered here. We have to protect our vision."

Abraham de Loor presents me only with a flight of fancy. He uses words well yet none of them is entirely convincing. They are just mirages on the horizon. We all experiment with our own fantasies. He speaks only of an idealized dream, a sense of reality is missing. The earth is not felt. The sea is too far distant, and the sky is not recognized either. I answer:

"Petrus Nel doesn't think like you, and no fine tradition

informs him. He's a dour Calvinist, so Jehovah, and the eye for an eye and a tooth for a tooth morality, influences him. He's a bigot and aggressive. He would not speak these words."

Abraham de Loor rejects me and insists on defending Petrus Nel. I am shocked by his blindness as I listen to another eulogy about the Afrikaner.

"You are guilty too, with that English mistrust of the Boers. You disparage Petrus Nel. You live among us, and yet you also remain apart. You are English and you never let us forget it. We are a simple people who are Calvinists and hard working. We have our own moral standards and insist on law and order. This rape is more than a threat. It's not just another Kaffir attack on the laager. It's even more serious. Black men seducing white women. The corruption of the Afrikaner nation and the begetting of a brown race. Petrus Nel sees this. New Kimberly is on the defensive. I don't agree, and think this rape is an isolated incident. Make allowances for the Boers. You should get out. The Coloured will survive. Bastards are tough, and he's a mongrel. You are a woman, and no one will criticize."

"Braam! Braam! We torment one another, and must not argue like this. It's so wrong. We are good friends. I need your help."

"Forgive me, Christina. The rape exposes all our sensitivities."

We sit in a helpless silence, and are contrite. We are grown-up people and should not behave like undisciplined children. Marius Greyling arrives and saves us from our shared sense of embarrassment. Abraham de Loor rises and introduces this young advocate.

"Christina, meet Marius Greyling. He's just returned from Leyden."

"I'm glad to meet you, Miss Ransome."

Auburn hair circles his face like a pale halo. He is a man of a winter disposition with an inward eye of introspection. I suspect that he might indeed be that new Afrikaner, the "Renaissance man" in Africa. His years in Europe would have allowed him the cultivation of that idealistic impulse. Perhaps he now returns to restore an old order here. He may indeed have the means to repulse the new barbarians. He fills me with hope. I speak:

"I'm glad you've come. We need your help. I hope you'll take the case."

Marius Greyling nods. He is not easily snared, as he answers:

"I cannot promise an acquittal."

Abraham de Loor makes his apologies and leaves. He knows my need for privacy, as this rape allegation presents delicate areas. Marius Greyling drubs on the table with long bony fingers, and I could easily imagine a lute in those hands. I avoid his intense and probing look. Instead, I gaze toward the Lootsberg mountains. I say:

"You will miss Leyden."

I remember Leyden so clearly, with its Dutch gabled houses, and the land is flat and dun-colored and the sea is always a threat. There's a blue washed sky and the poplars bend under the wind. Many rare and precious manuscripts are preserved at Leyden University. Marius Greyling's eyes hold this wisdom, and he hasn't squandered this pearl of the Medicis among the surly Boers. He survives even in the intractable Karoo. He speaks:

"I will miss Leyden University. Holland was my refuge. The library at Leyden was magnificent. I remember those incredible manuscripts, and that often the papyrus crumbled between my fingers. I learned to understand something of Egyptian hiero-glyphics, Aramaic, and even Sanskrit texts. I felt such a reverence for the past when I touched ancient history that was still pre-served in those fragments of parchment. Yet, this excitement faded, and I just wanted to come home. I needed to witness the severe beauty of the Karoo again. I wanted to grip a hand axe, or observe the endurance of a thorn tree. These are my reasons for returning. A great war has just devastated Europe, and there's no reclaiming the past. We've got to think of the future . . ."

I understand that Marius Greyling undergoes a transformation. He's fired in the same crucible as Abraham de Loor, and yet he's gone even further than my old friend. He asks the real questions. I hope that Ebrahim will make the same journey, but the location is a crueler background, and there's little beauty there. The dark and dismal hills, and the veld's gray stubble of grass. The offal and the excrement multiply. The Karoo's grandeur goes unseen, and Ebrahim suffers the hardship of this barren vision. Yet the seed of a European heritage is also possible here. This bloom flowers in Marius Greyling, and struggles for life in Abraham de Loor, and is still dormant in Ebrahim.

"So you did return here. I've had the same experience. I took the grand tour of Europe, and saw the museums of Italy, and witnessed the ruins of Pompeii. I recognized the statuary of Greece as perfect athletes frozen in perpetuity. I experienced a seduction of the gods. It's the same temptation . . ."

"Yet something is still missing, as if we've needed to find another dimension to living. That's reason for returning to Africa. I lived through this war in Europe and I chose to be a conscientious objector. A new army of Pagans threatened civilization. It wasn't just the Germans, but another darkness spewed forth filth, and a pus-filled cyst burst. I mean hatred, violence and slaughter. These contagions infected us, and so the many battles were fought. Now it is over, and Europe is a cemetery. There are those crosses and the nameless graves. Yet, this historical purification is necessary too. I know it's a bleak vision, and those echoes of war resound in me. The outer spectacle of carnage remains too. That's really why I came home. I need to escape the sight of death. The air of Africa is so clear, and the landscape is so still. The solitude is immense, I heal here. I'm sorry . . . I didn't mean to afflict you with my problems."

"Please, I do understand. You've lived through a holocaust."

His frankness is reassuring and I share his horror of war and senseless carnage. We have this compassionate view in common. He turns his attention to me now. He asks:

"Tell me about yourself . . ."

"There are similarities between us. I returned to Africa, and felt as you did. I'd been energized by Europe, and the ruins of Pompeii, and the art of Florence. Those art treasures moved me, and I was matured by these antiquities. Yet I discovered that learning was not like flaunting a jewel, but rather like using a tool. I'm a woman and I should like jewels but I don't care for diamonds or rubies or even emeralds. I prefer the feel of a hoe, or a spade. There are also the tools of the mind, and they are the best in the end. I needed something real, and I wanted to find my hands full. It wasn't only intellectual. The heart too felt that something was missing. Tolstoy filled me with longing. He strove after a new society, and went further than Rousseau's belief in the 'noble man.' I had a true need to divest myself. I was in a ferment and had so many ideas. Yet none of them gelled . . ."

"Please continue. I've heard that you were a follower of Gandhi. You must tell me about him. He's a man who knows about peace, and it's a necessity in our time."

I sense my own reservations. His plea is sincere, yet there are private areas to my relationship with Gandhi. I was and am still his disciple. Gandhi is the most important influence in my life, yet it's Kasturbai that I worry about. She walks in his shadow, and is somehow diminished. It's not only being a Hindu wife, but it's also her acceptance of a half-life. I recognize this and I've not been able to warn her. She's handed me a bowl of lentils, and I've smiled and thanked her. There's been nothing to challenge. Kasturbai's an orderly person, a disciplined saint, who obeys instinctively. Generations of child-brides speak with her tongue. These children who are ruled by their husbands. She serves others first. She waits on Gandhi, and then on myself, and attends to the other ashramites too. She masks her hidden pain, and poses as the "good wife." She's no such person. I dare not question her motive. Instead, I must talk about Gandhi.

"Africa summoned me and I came home. Then I met Gandhi. He was holding a meeting at the Hamidia Mosque in Johannesburg, and I went there alone. It was more out of a real need than any curiosity. I had a sense of expectancy too, and didn't know just what lay ahead. Yet I was filled with hope . . ."

I pause, as that sense of apprehension mingled with elation returns to me now. The memory of my meeting with Gandhi at the Hamidia Mosque is still clear. That was the night of the pass burning. My head still spins, and my hands tremble, and I have a sense of light. It's got nothing to do with Europe's sun, that reflects the glint of its art treasures. There's no suggestion of the power of conquest. This was an experience of Asia. That night convinced me of the truth of *ahimsa*. This is a teaching of the Hindu scriptures, and it's a message danced by Shiva. The luminous nature of the mind is revealed, as the natural goodness of the self unfolds. It is like the lotus flower that rises out of the filth and mud of India, and shines with a pure transparency. Gandhi changed my life that day, and I wonder if that power for the good is still possible in my life now.

"Tell me about the man . . ."

"Yes, I'll try and explain as clearly as I can. He was a 'boatman,' one who—according to Hindu scripture—ferries others to a farther shore. He possessed remarkable powers. I recall that the Hamidia Mosque was packed that evening. The crowd was seething with a pent-up excitement. Muslims in green turbans, and white jodhpur pants, mingled with Hindus in colored robes, while the richer merchants affected Western dress, and wore top hats and frock coats. The effect was quite strange, and they looked so provincial. Gandhi took the platform, and immediately commanded attention. He insisted on talking to these small businessmen, who were greedy and mean. They were hard-fisted peasants, and feared for their tenure here. They were the Indian immigrants who had come to Natal as indentured laborers. They still felt like slaves, and knew nothing about freedom . . ."

I pause, as I recall those cringing and nervous men. I can still see their anxious faces. They communicated their fears. They were no fierce Gurkhas. They held no remote outpost. The

Muslims had already invaded India, as happened in the sixth century. Hinduism luckily extends itself so that every fabric of another culture becomes an eye or arm of Shiva. Gandhi knew this and refused to accept their defeat. He used his immense spiritual energies and forced a change in these miserable peasants. Marius Greyling allows me this pause. Yet he too is anxious for a resolution. He finally insists:

"Don't keep me in suspense. Tell me what happened next?"

"He told them to burn their registration certificates."

"Did they burn the passes?"

"Yes, they did. Gandhi succeeded with his demand. A wailing sound filled the Mosque, and it was both a cry of triumph and a bellow of fear. Those merchants and shopkeepers rose to their feet, and moved like a herd of stampeding animals, as they cried out: 'Burn the registration certificates! Burn the registration certificates. We refuse to carry these passes.' Their faces showed different expressions. Greedy and self-satisfied men were outraged, and resented both Gandhi and Smuts. Now they were forced to make a choice. Others writhed in indecision, or were trapped by their fear. Cowardice marked other faces. A thin fakir man drew his own blood with a knife. Others implored Allah, and bowed toward Mecca. They wailed too. Many held back and refused to commit themselves for they feared breaking the law. Gandhi begged a second time, and then all surrendered. Not a single man held back, as hands dug into pockets and the hated registration certificates were exposed. The wound was revealed: Indians were forced to carry passes like Blacks. This was a cauterizing experience. Gandhi had exposed and touched that pain. He forced this agony upon them. With a cry, men hurled their passes into the fire. I watched like a spectator, for this was a scene out of history. It was the first cry of REVOLUTION. My eyes brimmed with tears, and then it was over. The hated registration certificates were all burnt. Even the fire had gone out, and each man was like a cinder. I hadn't burned a pass. I didn't carry one, because I was white, a European of South Africa. Gandhi noticed me, and invited me with his eyes.

I became the victim of a strange seduction. His gaze penetrated me, and I felt a stabbing in the heart. I was suddenly stripped of all pretense, and it seemed as if the layers of ignorance fell away. I saw a pure void rise up, and a lotus floated there in space. The petals were golden, and it swam before me. I felt as if I were elsewhere. Then I faced Gandhi's piercing gaze, as he smiled and pressed his hand over mine. I felt his power then, and it was crystallized in this gift, a small sesame seed. I understood the meaning of a renounced heart, and a sense of peace. I immediately became a *satyagrahi*, a passive resister, and took up the struggle."

Marius Greyling has heard me now, and there's nothing more to tell about Gandhi. I'm drained by the recounting of that experience, as it is still very precious. Marius Greyling does appreciate my story, as he smiles, and applauds with a real gratitude.

"I envy you this experience, Miss Ransome. Leyden pales in comparison. You talk of a living text, and a real experience. Clutch onto your precious sesame seed, and never allow it to shrivel and die. Few people have this opportunity, so don't waste it. I wish I'd had your luck. You've lived out incredible years. Yet you seem lost in this Karoo dorp."

He is less that sensitive Renaissance man now, and assumes the role of a clever prosecutor. I too am changing. Those idealistic years spent with Gandhi were not entirely noble. There are other elements too that cannot be ignored. I see the dark face of Kasturbai. Gandhi reads a passage from the scriptures. She shuffles off, and her sandals flop in the sand. She sits quietly under a tree, and fans herself, and brushes away flies. Her face is impassive, and I just don't understand. I wonder if she doubts God. I don't dare question whether she loves her husband. It's not an important consideration for an Indian woman. She does her duty, and attends to Gandhi's needs. She serves others. She'll die in peace. I recall her unspoken suffering, as I try and put my hands on my own life.

"Those were the difficult years. I was committed to the struggle for political change, and took part in strikes protest marches. I even believed that a revolution was taking place. Yet I was bewildered too. I even admit that my devotion to Gandhi was tested, but this had nothing to do with his public image, or dedication to passive resistance. It was my own sense of the shadows thrown by his private life. His marriage was a strange enigma, and nobody really understood it. He married Kasturbai when they were both children in India. He was a Hindu husband, and she was a child-bride. Yet even within this context of bizarre self-indulgence, there were further contradictions. Gandhi took the path of a disciplined yogi, and chose finally to remain celibate. This choice is not surprising within the tradition of Indian life. Yet for Westerners the matter of Gandhi's troubled marriage was confusing. Kasturbai became a kind of widow, and I sympathized with her. Yet, Gandhi remained my mentor, and I valued my relationship with him. Finally, my ambivalence became a strain. The problem was further complicated when I fell in love with an Indian. Sanjay Pillay was not a follower of Gandhi, even though his parents had come here as indentured laborers from Madras. We lived together in Durban, and I conceived his child. Then, I had a miscarriage, and lost that child. Sanjay died too, of a heart attack. I felt totally destroyed, and believed that I'd made all the wrong choices. I went into exile in the remote Karoo. I wanted time to think, and I also needed a second chance."

I refuse to counterfeit flesh and bone, and deliberately give only the bare facts. I will not resurrect Sanjay again, even though it is Ebrahim who dances before me. I insist that this love is a private matter. I can still recall Sanjay's naked body, as if I had dismembered him in a dream. I again hold a thigh; the palm of a hand; a delicate ankle; a soft and moist mouth; an eye with its capacity for beauty; a squirming tongue like a fish; the hardness of the groin and the erect member. Nothing of this escapes me. Sanjay's power and uniqueness remain, and can never be duplicated. Ebrahim is different, yet there is a resemblance between them. I struggle for words:

"What does it mean? The past is gone, swept out to sea, and strong currents carry it elsewhere. I see this love washed up on a strange beach, and it's picked at by birds, and gobbled up by fish, and gnawed at by dogs, and then bleached by the sun. It's just blown away, and now it's gone . . . gone . . . gone."

"Take your time. Memories can be painful . . ."

Marius Greyling is right. Those memories of our days spent together on the Natal coast return, and they linger in my mind. There are limpid images as I recall the soft sand underfoot. Our bodies drowned then in our fierce embrace. The sea of love carried us toward dangerous shoals. Storms rose up on the horizon, and we foundered on the rocks. We sank like stones, and drifted, if at all, like the life at the bottom of the ocean. Crabs scuttled there, and barnacled snouts of fish blundered out of holes. We were hurt, and broken. We took up our separate lives again. My child was dislodged too, and it's as if that same wild sea caused my miscarriage. These memories are hard to bear, and my voice rises again.

"I lost that child, and I still can't believe it, even now. Yet, I saw that the blood refused to pulse, and recognized that the mind was still unformed. The cruel sea dislodged it like that stone. Creation's breath failed in its work, and I can still hardly believe it."

Marius Greyling is sympathetic, and does not think me guilty of any weakness. He speaks in a supportive tone of voice.

"Please, I don't question your pain."

"I do . . ."

"Make an end to this suffering."

"Why should I?"

"I need to know about Ebrahim . . ."

"Mr. Greyling, in talking about my own child, I reflect my love and concern for Ebrahim. Try and understand my words in this light. I've told you that my child miscarried. He was born before his time, not only in the womb, but also in history. He would not have been accepted in South Africa, and the Boers would have rejected him too. He'd also have been a Coloured. I'm an English woman and Sanjay Pillay was an Indian. He'd have been a pariah, an Untouchable among Brahmin Boers. I'd have found that situation intolerable, so I'm not sorry about that miscarriage. He'd be better off to choose a wiser age for his birth. My son would survive in the twenty-first century. Then, there might be a golden age, after revolution, a time of sages and their wise dispensation. Now, he would face only suffering and despair."

"Please go on . . ."

"Ebrahim was like a son, and replaced that child that I lost in the miscarriage. I'm like a mother to him. He's no criminal, and he didn't rape that Boer girl. Ebrahim loved her. She's simple-minded and that's the pity. The Boers will never believe it. The old bogey man of miscegenation still lurks in the shadows, and that's the scarecrow of Afrikanerdom. It's a terrifying sight at night, but in the day it's just a wooden figure with a pumpkin head. I know, because I loved an Indian and suffered the nightmare of being caught in bed with him. My nakedness would have seemed like a blasphemy, and I could have found myself like a lover being driven out of paradise. I might have become another wild Eve who cursed the night. Thank God it never happened to me. Ebrahim suffers now because of their attitude toward miscegenation. He is cursed, and the Boers damn him in the name of love. We both need your help, Mr. Greyling. Please take this case and defend him against the Boers . . ."

"Tell me about the rape."

"There was no rape."

"Tell me what happened."

I see that Marius Greyling has become the relentless prosecutor. His face is no longer noble, and does not resemble that Renaissance man in Africa. Instead, he's regressed and joins the Boers of New Kimberly. He's content to be just another Goth or Vandal who rides in for the kill. The high peaks of the Lootsberg exhort me to speak the truth and my words will sound that crystal gong.

"There was no rape."

"I want to believe you . . ."

"There was no rape. Ebrahim was attracted to Sannie de Bruyn. I had sent him to her parents' house with a message. So their encounter was not surprising. He's a handsome youth, and romantic, with a love of poetry. The girl was naturally drawn to him. She's retarded but it made no difference. Rather, it was an asset. She did not withdraw from him, and didn't notice his skin color. She saw only his beauty. Her parents were busy, and her sisters were grown up, so Ebrahim was an exciting playmate. The girl had a wagon, clay oxen and two black dolls. They all went off on a journey together. The wagon rolled across the bed and there were exciting adventures. It was all in the game. Sannie got excited, and Ebrahim enjoyed the fun. Children endure such tension, and Ebrahim held her close for reassurance. An intimacy took place, a love between a man and a woman. He didn't rape the girl. It was a seduction. There, I've told you, and I hope that I've not perjured myself . . ."

I feel ashamed. I have indeed perjured myself in talking about the intimate life of another. I feel almost like an approving partner in this seduction. Marius Greyling senses my inner turmoil, and insists:

"Miss Ransome, I admire your courage: you are a brave woman. I believe you that there was no rape of the Boer girl. I agree that the boy probably seduced her. None of this helps our case. The Coloured will go to prison. It's still an ugly charge."

I feel so exhausted, as images pass through my mind. I see again my unborn child; Sanjay with his gracious good looks; Gandhi and his firm intention to do only good; Kasturbai and her silent and unspoken pain; and then Ebrahim, with his haggard face and accusing eyes. I answer:

"So, it's all just hopeless. I should have guessed it. Ebrahim won't survive a long prison sentence: he'll come out a different person. He won't even be a shadow of his former self. He'll alter and become an oaf or an idiot or an animal. He could even ape his jailers: he's capable of becoming a tyrant, too."

Marius Greyling does not tolerate either his weakness, or my own, but insists on our solidarity. He speaks in a firm voice and rouses me so that I recover my own lost identity. He returns me to my old definition of myself: a *satyagrahi*, a member of a classless society, a dedicated revolutionary.

"It's never easy. Don't surrender to your struggle with doubt, but remember that the law is not inviolate. It can be twisted, and then the innocent suffer while the guilty go free. There's no true justice in any society. That's an undertaking for the gods, rather than men. Still, I am taking this case. There will be no fee, you must attend to the bail money. We'll challenge miscegenation. It's an evil prejudice, but we will not win any allies. The boy is the catalyst, and he will be sacrificed. That's the price you pay. I need your support in this plea for decency."

Marius Greyling is right. I cannot save Ebrahim, and must be prepared to sacrifice him. Gandhi taught me this. He sacrificed Kasturbai and left her barren and powerless. He took his semen elsewhere and fathered the *satyagraha*, the militant passive resisters. They are his children and I am his revolutionary daughter. Kasturbai was like a servant. She looked after him, and her singlemindedness left her useless. She had no other task. He waxed and waned like a moon shining as she fell out of the sky. She was a shooting star. One life fed upon another, and it's happening again now. I'm edging Ebrahim out of the constellation. His planets are out of alignment, and he will fall from grace. I will rise again, with a new ascendancy. Self-sacrifice will make me nubile again. The Hindu scriptures declare: "The way to salvation is narrow, like crossing the sharp edge of a razor."

o   o   o

There are mirages everywhere, and cities appear on the horizon; Florence with its spires and domes, St. Peter's vault in Rome, the statuary of Greece, and the paintings of the Uffizi Gallery are all strewn about the Karoo. Even New Kimberly is just another mirage. It's hard to grasp the truth any more, as rumor and distortion always precede a time of revolution.

Ebrahim is free; he's out on bail. The angry lion is loose, and he rages in my house now. His curls are gone. They shaved his head, and he looks like a convict. The olive luster to his complexion is absent too. He's an Untouchable now, and belongs in the location. He snarls like an angry dog.

"Don't stare at me. I know what I look like, and I'm not asking for pity."

"Don't say that. I only want to help."

"Nothing helps. I've got a long memory, and I'll get those bastards. They came at me with a razor, and Cronje held me down and threatened: 'You won't fuck a white girl again.' Van Aswegen was savage too, as he said: 'Next time, we'll cut off your balls.' They meant it, too. I swore and Cronje's hand tightened on the razor."

"They shouldn't have done that."

"What do you know?"

Ebrahim rages, like a cornered animal. He spits and the gob of mucous glistens.

"I want to help. Please let me . . ."

He sits, and the anger drains away. He's suddenly like a flaccid balloon. Then, the anguish and the remorse set in as he whispers his apologies.

"I'm sorry, Miss Ransome, I shouldn't have said these things to you. It's just that I hate myself. I've become ugly."

"That's not true. You are Ebrahim . . . you are my Italian boy . . ."

"It's true, I am different . . . a hot-not . . . a bastard . . . a Capie . . . the white man's shit . . . that part about himself which he hates. I belong in the location. I shouldn't have come here. You and this house are part of my old life. Now everything is in ruins . . . it's all gone."

He must not diminish his life, because nothing is over. He is still intact, and he will survive even here in the Karoo. Other things continue. The aberrant life of the veld proliferates. There are the steady rocks, and the serene mountains. I survive here, because I've become tough, and he can do the same. I speak:

"I agree that you've suffered. The warders are like beasts and they've been vicious toward you. The Boers are responsible, but you've got to survive the pain and ugliness. We all struggle in the Karoo, and I've buckled here too. I'm not the same person. Some aspect of myself is angry, and I endure out of a deep-seated bitterness. Yet, I still hope for the miracle of a rebirth, and you must do the same. Don't dismiss this chance, because miracles can and do happen. Keep your head clear, and then you won't explode and wreck everything. That would be a mistake. The trial is still ahead."

My words are useless, and he refuses even to consider them. He feels blocked, and threatened, and sees no way out. There are obstacles everywhere, and they litter his path. The vine bangs against the window as he announces, in a sober voice:

"I won't stand trial."

"What do you mean . . . ?"

"You heard me."

This is a betrayal: he must not jump bail. I gave Marius Greyling my word, and now Ebrahim lets me down. Our defense is more important than his grab at freedom, and I must insist that he stand trial.

I have a sense of his desolation, and that this arid land oppresses him. He feels as if he's swallowed burning stones, and he finds only scorpions underfoot. Even now, his head is reared like a cobra and ready to strike.

"Don't you see that I'd be destroyed? Another prison experience would kill me. I don't stand a chance. I raped a white girl: that's the charge. I even believe it, and I've become obscene too. Why don't you spit on me? That's all I'm worth. I disgust even myself."

"Stop it! You are self-indulgent."

"What do you know? You are a white woman."

"That's an unjust remark. I'm only trying to help."

He writhes inwardly, as if aware of slime on his body. He whispers:

"You make me feel guilty, and I owe you so much."

"You owe me nothing, other than your honesty."

"I don't hate you."

"I know that."

"It's those others. The bastards are everywhere. The whole world is against me. Nobody is on my side, not even you, Miss Ransome."

I deny that he is so rejected. He does have a place in society, and he must claim it. He must not slink away like an Untouchable. He is no pariah, even though he returns to the location.

"This is nonsense. You do have friends, so don't give in to despair. Now just listen to me. I've briefed an advocate, Marius Greyling. He's a liberal and very sympathetic, and he will defend you. There'll be no acquittal. You do face a long prison sentence, and you've got to be brave about it. There's no running away. Miscegenation is an evil. Society should be totally open, and the races should be able to mix freely. This is our chance to say this. The cruelty and hypocrisy of this land must be challenged."

He interjects with a raucous laugh.

"I'm not one of your causes . . ."

"Please, I didn't mean it like that . . ."

"I'm saving my own skin. Prison has taught me about survival, and I'm getting the hell out of here. Fuck any court case. I won't stand trial."

I listen, and his words don't surprise me. I didn't think he'd play along with any of this. He's running, and he's always been running. He ran from the location to my house. He ran from my house to the Boer girl, and now he runs from New Kimberly. He runs just as far as he needs to go, and he's moving further and further away from people. Kasturbai also ran, but not in the physical sense. She moved slowly, with the stately steps of a tall woman in a sari. She walked a few paces, and then she squatted in the sun. Her hands brushed away flies. Yet, she was still running. Her eyes were distant, and they reflected nothing; no Indian sunrise, no African sunset. She was elsewhere. I watched her shadow, and it was different. It was like a tame dog, and kept up with the long, loping stride of Gandhi. The real Kasturbai was an exile, a pair of eyes watching. She abdicated from life and chose to stand on the side-lines. She is just a presence, like a stone. She insists on this anonymity, and she has her own reasons. Ebrahim has no excuse. I answer:

"You've got to stand trial . . ."

He wavers for a moment with indecision. He is not Kasturbai, and he doesn't possess her intuition. He's also a political prisoner. He's being tried for love and the right for people to live together, irrespective of their color or race. He's in a position to strike a blow for true liberty if he agrees to stand trial. Instead, he's overwhelmed with misery, and replies:

"They threatened to cut off my balls . . ."

"They didn't mean it."

"They hate me . . ."

"That isn't true either . . ."

"I've had a white girl, and they hate me. I won't go back to prison, and I refuse to be mutilated. I am a man, and I have dignity."

These are only vile threats. South Africa is a civilized country, people are not castrated here. There have been difficulties: those evils that were perpetuated during the Boer War; the traitors who were tried and shot in kangaroo military courts; prisoners who were ill-treated; Boer women and children who suffered in the British concentration camps. These were all inhuman acts, and they must not happen again. Lessons are learned in any war. I try and reassure Ebrahim.

"Listen to me. The warders are not the authorities. Your safety is important, and that's their responsibility. These are ugly threats and nothing more. Don't give in to them, and don't allow the Boers to win. They must not control your mind. Then you would have reason for anxiety."

Ebrahim is not reassured. He's like a man who's being pursued. He sees vultures circle in the sky, and hears the lynx snarl close by. The desolate Karoo instils this delirium, and he's unable to fight it off. Panic adds a note of hysteria to his voice.

"I am not mistaken. Cronje still carries a knife, and it will be sharp as a razor. It won't be my hair this time, it will be my balls. Cursing won't save me. There is no God in heaven, and there never was one. There is no law there. I've had a white girl, and the Boers hate that worst of all. They become like mad dogs, and they form a pack. Then, they ride out with guns, and they hunt a man down, and think of him only as a jackal. There is no protection. Love is no help, and even bravery is absurd. I've forgotten Sannie. Her white body is obscene. She is just a cheap whore, and love is a dirty word. The Boers are riding now, their voices angry. They have bloodshot eyes, and shake their huge fists. They never give up. They close in for the kill. Don't you hear? The Boers are already here, and they are moving outside."

"Stop it! Do you hear me? Enough of this melodrama. None of this will ever happen. South Africa is a civilized country, and the Boers are not evil men. You are hysterical. Try and calm down and control yourself. Otherwise, you will make yourself ill. You are precious to me, and I cannot bear the thought of losing you. The trial must take place. We are in this together, and I will not desert you. Ebrahim, try and trust me."

My plea succeeds, as I watch the terror drain from his face. His personality appears to alter, as his mood dramatically changes. He is even magnetic, and the cropped head is no longer disfiguring. Instead, a mature man replaces the turbulent boy. His manner leaves me bewildered. He's become more sophisticated, and sure of himself, but I'm also aware of a disturbing vanity. I speak carefully.

"You seem more relaxed. I'm glad that you've calmed down. You even appear confident."

He struggles momentarily with confused emotions, which cloud his face, and he speaks.

"No, you don't understand. It's more than just confidence. You confessed that I was precious to you. That changes everything. You must know this, I love you, Christina. Now I will even stand trial, because the future is worthwhile. The past is only a nightmare. The miracle has happened. Your love will sustain me now."

I cannot reply. Yet this declaration of love is really no surprise. I already guessed it when I saw the look of desire that was so often reflected in his face during our classes, but I chose to ignore these warning signs, and now it is too late. There are so many obstacles too; the Boers and their wrath, Ebrahim and the Boer girl, and then Lakshmi's presence swims before me. The net of illusion tightens; Kali, the destroyer, presides now, and we are all her victims. The truth is that Ebrahim is in serious trouble, and I must give him a sober answer.

"Listen to me. I respect your feelings. They are a young man's romantic dreams. I am a good friend, and can't be anything more. You will understand when you are older. The Boers threaten us, and they are out for vengeance. We are in a dangerous situation. There's no time for sentiment."

My words fail to discourage him. Instead, he's even more consumed by passion. He leans over and undoes my bun, and my hair cascades down over my shoulders. I am taken unawares, and feel suddenly young, and desire him too. The shock of it throws me off my guard. He takes advantage of this opportunity, and forces a kiss, and his hands travel across my breasts. He whispers with a renewed ardor:

"Christina, throw away your constraints and don't mourn any longer for your Indian lover. He's gone, and I am here now. I want to care for you. Admit that you love me. I know that you do, because I've seen the way you look at me. This moment is precious. Out time together could be short, so let's not delay. You must trust me."

I push away his arms, and turn my head, and avoid his lips. I don't look into his dark, seductive eyes. Lakshmi divides us, and flows between us like an impassable river. There is no avoiding this obstacle. She carries the secret of love between her thighs, and Ebrahim made this journey when he seduced the Boer girl. The burden of this knowledge is too great. I refuse to surrender to his erotic charms.

"Please! You offend me. I am not your paramour. I'm twenty years older than you, and that's another kind of chasm. It's a chance I won't take. There's a parental bond too, and I think of you as a son. Anything else is incestuous."

He refuses to listen to me. He continues to press kisses on my hands. His mouth is soft and moist as a swimming fish. I recall other such moments when Sanjay knelt above me. The universe disappeared, with the cessation of shape and form, and I saw my ego vanquished. There was nothing at all at my center, just the total bliss of the moment. He is importunate.

"Please, Christina, our moment may not come again. Love could be too late for us. We must not let that happen. Just confess your love for me, and then we will be together. That's all that I ask."

"Leave me alone. There is no time left; it's too late. You seduced a white girl. The Boers see only this rape. They will not be appeased and want your blood. You need me as a mother, and I can serve you best in that role. Please leave now. Keep off the streets."

"You choose to play games, and I understand. These are a woman's wiles. You'll soon get tired of it, because all games become boring. Don't leave it too late. The Boers will make life difficult, you are right about that. We must not squander this love. That would be unforgivable."

"Get out."

He strolls out of the room, and he's like a dark angel. He'll move like a shadow into the night, and the location will claim him. The moon will favor him, she'll obliterate his tracks. He'll sleep safely tonight. My shadow moves in another direction. I follow Kasturbai. She walks out into the hot Indian sun, and sits under a shady tree. Ahmedabad is distant, and the city glowers. She sits alone, and I beseech her impassive eyes, for I need her help. Kasturbai smiles. Cleopatra had such a smile, and it's the look of queens and regents. Kasturbai is a regent, and Gandhi is a king. Her shadow follows him. It's like a dog. She keeps up with him, and follows that long, loping stride. She moves like a thin black line. Gandhi grows huge. He's a holy man, a mahatma. He's become a vehicle for salvation, and she is still a shadow.

o   o   o

The Lootsberg flaunt a white-capped grandeur, and only recently winds lashed the summit. The arctic wastes are there. I see clouds darken the horizon, and the sky turns the color of steel. The elements humble us. Yet the veld prepares for spring, as the grasses show new white plumes. I am taken by surprise when Abraham de Loor calls. The old man is visibly agitated.

"Get ready at once. Things have changed; the situation has deteriorated. You must leave immediately."

"Is there more trouble?"

"The Boer girl is pregnant."

I'm left speechless by this news, but it shouldn't have come as a surprise to learn that this game of love between Ebrahim and the Boer girl will now be sanctified by a child. Yet the Boers will curse it. I answer softly.

"So, there's going to be a child . . ."

"Yes, a black baby . . ."

"Forget about any notion of racial purity. We both know that Van Riebeeck's men took Hottentot women as their common-law wives."

"There's no doubt. The doctor confirms the pregnancy. Now there will really be trouble."

"I know. The Boers will not let the matter rest. They'll curse this offspring. They'll hound Ebrahim, I'll be smeared too, and my good name is worthless here. Things couldn't be any worse."

"The dorp is seething, the Boers want vengeance. You are in deep trouble. You are attached to this Coloured. You've paid the bail money, and you've arranged for his defense, and he's let you down. We all make mistakes. Christina, get out. Things are moving fast, and I fear reprisals . . ."

"What are you saying?"

"You are welcome at 'Bergzicht.' "

He's avoiding the real issue. I know that trouble brews in the dorp. I too dream of "Bergzicht," where the mountains tower close to the farm. Those buttresses assume their own fantastic shapes, and stairways and terraces appear in stone. A miniature Parthenon exists within the Lootsberg. Other parapets and ramparts rise up out of an even older past when the barbarians of prehistory occupied this fortress. Those battle cries still echo and interrupt the mountain's silence. Yet I refuse to be deflected. Gandhi will ring that crystal gong, and it will sound on, and on, beyond the sound of rifle fire. The mountain has its cadence. I answer firmly:

"My place is here."

"That's ridiculous."

"Ebrahim needs me."

A vine trembles outside, and we both listen, as if we expect something to shatter. The wind is a marauder in the garden. The sun's pale light gives the Lootsberg a rare transparency, and the mountains float like distant icebergs. He speaks:

"Christina, please reconsider my offer. It still holds. You'll be safer at 'Bergzicht.' The dorp is troubled and anything could happen."

"I've made up my mind. I'm staying."

"You are stubborn."

"It's a question of conscience."

"Christina, men must settle this dispute. Leave it to the Boers. Matters must take their course now. I might even be mistaken, and the situation could calm down. There might even be no violence. But you are a woman, and you are alone. Don't you understand that you must come with me?"

"No, Braam. I refuse to leave, and I will not be silenced. I'm staying here. My place is with Ebrahim and he needs my help. There's no one else."

"It will do you no good."

I'm so weary of men with their persistent good advice. First, there was Gandhi and his promise of an austere salvation, and then Sanjay with his oriental dreams of power and love. Now Abraham de Loor offers me some good, old-fashioned paternal advice. I want nothing from any of them. I've become indifferent to men and their demands. I think of Kasturbai. She made no demands. She took the brunt of it all. She traveled far within herself, and came to understand her own life. She developed the ability to be still. She was content.

"Braam, I've thought it over. I've got to stand by Ebrahim."

"Be rid of him. This Coloured is a criminal, and a leech on your life. Men must settle this dispute. Learn from the Boer women. They are patient wives, and know their duty. You are no different."

"I don't need examples."

"I think you do."

"The Boer women are in purdah."

"That's enough."

Abraham de Loor bridles at my words. I recall Kasturbai's struggle, which was also Gandhi's battle. I need their wisdom, and his dark eyes blaze, even in memory. I'm almost taken in by his just anger, but I haven't reckoned with Kasturbai's struggle. She moves here, and I glimpse her green and gold sari. I recall her plea for freedom now, because it's mine too, when I take on men like Abraham de Loor. Kasturbai wanted to join in the struggle, but Gandhi was a reluctant spouse, and argued that women are no revolutionaries. He feared that the weaker sex might flinch. Gandhi was a Hindu husband, and was assaulted by the images of temple walls. Shiva danced before him, and Kali trampled her consort in anger. He saw beyond the copulation of the gods, when he looked at Kasturbai and understood that his child-bride had already made her escape. She was a grown woman, who spoke her own mind. The battle was really his, but she was the victor. He could no longer ignore her cry for liberty. He surrendered, and freed his wife, and welcomed women as *satyagrahis*.

"Braam, please listen . . . I'm talking about women . . ."

"I feel sorry for you . . ."

"Braam, please. I'm not a child, or a concubine, or a patient wife. I am an emancipated woman, and I remember Zarina Cassim's fight for freedom. She was married according to Muslim custom and forced to wear a *burghan*, a hideous garment that hid her face, whenever she left the house. It was a Muslim rule that no man, other than her husband, should look upon her beauty. She too wanted to join the *satyagraha*, but her husband refused his permission. Gandhi stepped in, and settled the dispute. He debated with Mankir Cassim, and the Muslim quoted from the Koran. Muhammad favors men, and angels, but the Prophet has little interest in women. Gandhi did not fight alone, for Kasturbai's face implored him. She became his cause, and her newly-won freedom was like a seed. It was not the sesame seed, but a lotus flower, Kasturbai's own spiritual growth. Gandhi gave a discourse and spoke wisely upon the many virtues of women. He won the argument, and Mankir Cassim set his wife free. Zarina Cassim threw away the *burghan*, that imprisoning cloth, and allowed others to see her face. She was stunningly beautiful. She was also militant, and took up the struggle. Her freedom had just begun."

"This is a clever anecdote . . ."

"Please, don't reject my words."

"I do. This kind of talk is out of place. The Boers are a threat and you are in danger. You may be mad, but I am not. Please come with me to 'Bergzicht'."

"No, women have their rights. So many of them struggled, and I can remember Ayesha Padaychee. She had a strict father. He was poor and could not provide her with a dowry. He was an orthodox Hindu. Ayesha had her aspirations, and she too wanted to join the struggle. Aswin Padaychee refused his permission. Gandhi intervened, and Aswin Padaychee entrusted him with the interpretation of a prophetic dream in which the old man again loaded jute in the town of Serampore. The Hoogly River flowed past, and the early Danish settlers lay buried in the cemetery there. India was just the same, for nothing had altered; only Aswin Padaychee was different. He had aged, and he'd never load jute again. He would die in Africa, and the old man's eyes reflected this terror. Gandhi pacified his fears. He told him the truth, that there was no return to India, and that if the indentured laborers were to go free, protest and revolution were necessary. He revived the old man's faith in *ahimsa*. Aswin Padaychee died in peace, and let his daughter go. She joined the *satyagraha*. Ayesha was a brave woman."

"Have you finished?"

Abraham de Loor is impatient with my testimony. He sees these accounts of brave women as valueless, and they add nothing to his male-oriented view of history. He is not very different from Petrus Nel. Like him, Abraham de Loor will repeal no law, nor grant others their rights. He's blind as well as bigoted, and I'm right in believing justice is truly a woman.

"This is ridiculous. You distort the truth. Accept your frailty and know that we all make mistakes. Men and women are equal in their capacity for error. That's my judgment here, and it's a fair one."

"I'll do my best. I take my place in the world."

"We all do. It's not just you, or even women . . ."

"I fight my own battles . . ."

"I accept that . . ."

"All right, I agree to a truce . . ."

"You are welcome at 'Bergzicht'."

"Thank you . . ."

Abraham de Loor accepts my decision to remain in New Kimberly, so a truce is at last possible between us. He gravely examines my situation.

"The pregnancy alters things. The trial is too distant, and the Boers aren't prepared to wait. They want to settle scores. Their honor is at stake. We must be prepared."

"What do you mean?"

Abraham de Loor expresses his fears, and I see his anxieties are at last revealed. He speaks.

"There's talk of the *kommando* riding."

"I don't believe it."

I am stunned. I remember the Boer War, and those crack *kommando* units. They harassed the British army, and wore their own grim uniform. They dressed in black claw-hammer coats, and were as dark as night. They hid their features under broad-brimmed hats, and they were indeed the ministers of darkness. They were the angels of death. I still don't believe it's possible that the *kommando* will ride out tonight. Gandhi should shed tears here. He mourned for the war dead, and it must not happen again. The Boer War is over, and all hostilities should end.

"I'm not mistaken, Christina. These are Boer officers, twelve angry men. They are an unofficial jury and think God is on their side. Their horses are groomed, and their Mausers are primed. They will dispense justice."

"I don't believe it. No twelve citizens will ride out. It's just a rumor and nothing more. I know these men. They are my neighbors. Andres Perreira is sipping wine. Charl Myburg plays the piano, and enjoys Chopin. Jan Volschenk has put aside his meat cleaver, and hacks at a good joint of lamb. His aggression is no more than a desire for that succulent haunch. Basie Viviers plays cards, and always wins at bridge. Piet Burger is out hunting, and likes to bring down a buck. Wim Pieterse is writing letters. He's an excellent correspondent, and not among your *kommando*. Piet Barnard is interviewing a suitor for his daughter, and he's thinking more about a wedding than a funeral.

Ben Potgieter has gone fishing. He's caught eels often enough, when the river is low, and you'll find him there. Frans du Plessis blends tobacco, and enjoys his pipe. He's not there either. There's also Willem Goosen, a strange person. Yet, I cannot see him among your *kommando*. Petrus Nel! He's the demagogue. He's the incarnate form of war, and embodies that destructive energy. He cannot rest until this land explodes into violence. He is the leader of the *kommando*!"

My voice cracks on the edge of hysteria, as the *kommando* already takes shape in my imagination. The riders have the faces of beasts, for they are no longer men and have become animals. Jackals race across the veld now. Abraham de Loor tries to calm me, and insists:

"Christina, calm yourself. This is all speculation. I know that the *kommando* prepares, but I don't know their names. They are Boer officers, not outlaws. The dorp feels wronged, and the *kommando* wants vengeance. They will hunt the Coloured, but they will not bother you."

"Why do grown men hunt a boy?"

"I can lend you a revolver."

"No . . . no! No gun . . . no weapon."

"Men are often driven to violence."

"I'm glad I'm a woman . . ."

"This is an unhappy situation."

"It's a witch-hunt."

"Christina, it's useless to stay . . ."

"Braam, go home, go back to 'Bergzicht.' Your farm waits, and you can claim that silence, and even hold on to your peace of mind. Mine is shattered . . ."

Abraham de Loor leaves. He's grown older, and his face is ashen, while his eyes are dark holes. I've dealt harshly with him. Still, I have no regrets, and feel only pity toward him, and the Boers as well. I sense an eerie silence. He's right about the *kommando*. Those men will dress up in their claw-hammer coats, and fit on top hats. They will load Mauser rifles. They are crack shots, and have a license to kill.

I transcend this ugliness, and allow the mirages in. They float off the horizon. Sabarmati rises up and distant Ahmedabad glows. The river flows past, and the sacred cows wade there, while the pipal trees give their shade. My books hold their wisdom, and civilization is not lost. Gandhi is a distant figure, who debates with men. Brave Indian women adorn my life. The goddesses of temple walls, those child-brides, go to school. No man rules them now. Kasturbai smiles upon me.

o   o   o

Shipwreck washes him back up on my doorstep. The golden casket has split, and Ebrahim is back again. He is as dark as any of Moselikatse's warriors. The white child is no longer even a dream. He voices his distress.

"Men on horseback! They rode through the location, and fired into the air. They screamed: 'Hot-not! Bastard! We'll get you.' I ran for my life and kept off the streets. I stumbled across gardens, and climbed over fences. I'm bruised and my hands are lacerated. Dogs barked at me, and lamps shone in windows. I ran for my life and made it to your door. There's no place else for me to hide."

I ignore Abraham de Loor's admonition about harboring this young criminal. I only know that the *kommando* ride now and that they are without mercy. I'm forced to ask:

"What did they look like?"

Ebrahim is confused, and bewildered, and can't remember any details. He answers:

"I don't know. They all looked alike. It was dark, and they wore long black coats and they had broad-brimmed hats, as well as their guns and ammunition. They fired into the air, and I was their target."

He's useless. Dark men and powerful horses tell me nothing. He must be more specific. I need to know their names, if there is to be a reckoning.

"What did you see?"

"I've told you everything . . ."

"It's not enough. I must know more, so I'll prod your memory. Did you notice a swarthy man? He'd have had Latin features, and sat a horse well. That's Andres Perreira. I'm sure that he's not among this *kommando*. He's a decent man."

Ebrahim struggles against chaotic images that only further add to his confusion, and finally answers blankly:

"No. Nobody looked foreign. They were just Boers, and the usual ugly Dutchmen."

I must not allow his anger to cloud the facts. He must calm down, and think carefully.

"Take your time and try again. Did you notice a man wearing gold-rimmed spectacles? That could have caught your attention, and the lantern might have picked up the glint."

"No. There was no flash of gold. There were no spectacles either. They were ghouls. They had hollow eyes, that shone like live coals. They stared like jackals, and I ran from them . . ."

"Try and be sensible, and don't surrender to your own nightmares. Overcome these fears and think clearly. That's all that I ask."

"I'm trying my best . . ."

"I know. Did you notice a silver-handled riding crop?"

He bites his nails until the fingers bleed, and then fumbles for words:

"I don't know. I've told you everything. It was dark outside in the location. They carried lanterns but they gave a poor light. I didn't notice much. The Boers could have carried whips . . . or *sjamboks* . . . or axes. I only know that they were huge and filled the night. They would have beaten me and flogged me to death, if I had stayed around any longer. Don't you understand that I was running for my life . . . ?"

His confusion blurs everything, and it's of no help to me now. Yet I'm certain that he must remember some important detail which would identify the men of this *kommando*.

"Never mind, Wim Pieterse has that silver-handled riding crop. What about a cast in the eye?"

"What?"

"I'm talking about a squint."

"No. I saw nothing like that. I told you that they had no eyes, just burning coals. They could see in the dark, and I had to run very fast in order to escape them. I was a rat racing the darkness, and I moved so fast that they missed me. I hate them . . . the bastards . . . the fucking Boer bastards . . ."

He sweats and his eyes are red-rimmed. He sniffs too and wipes a nose that drips from anxiety, as I still insist that he must have noticed something.

"What about the butcher?"

"No. Nobody carried a meat cleaver."

"You are facetious."

"I've had enough. I've told you everything that I know, and there's nothing further I can add."

I ignore his discomfort. I'm only trying to help him, even though I sound like a cruel prosecutor. He must also learn preparedness because real-life courtroom dramas are like this. A jury would not only find him guilty but stupid too.

"What about a stutter?"

"I don't know."

"Frans du Plessis stutters . . ."

"I don't care."

"I do. It's important to this investigation. What about a high-sounding laugh like a woman's?"

Ebrahim stares at me in disbelief and thinks me really mad now. Yet, he must answer my question carefully, for I am the one who must draw the conclusions. He irks me: he's such an unreliable witness.

"Why do you mock me?"

"Just answer the question."

"No. They were men, and they had no women with them. There was no hope of mercy."

Kobus le Grange has a high voice, and sounds like a woman sometimes, particularly if he's excited or under stress. He obviously wasn't there. "What about a hacking cough?"

"Nobody coughed."

"A low whistle?"

"No. There was too much noise. The *kommando* was angry and men were shouting loudly."

We are making no progress. Ben Potgieter whistles and imitates bird calls, but he was certainly not there. Still, I won't give up, as I rack my brains and ask another question.

"A restless horse? A bad rider?"

"These men were soldiers. Their horses obeyed."

Ebrahim shows signs of strain. Still, I am the inquisitor, and must ignore his pale face and tense expression. His eyes accuse me of putting him on trial, but I must still persist with my questions.

"Did you notice a sly creature? He'd have been sniffing the night air. He'd be on the scent of any trouble, with sharp ears, and a pointed nose. He might even have been hard to see, for he can invent the darkness."

Ebrahim finds my words bewildering as he flatly states:

"They had no dog with them."

"I didn't mean an animal. This is a man. Willem Goosen. He's a tracker of the veld, and he learned this art from the Xhosa. He's not like a white man, but some kind of aberrant creature. Did you notice him?"

"I passed no such creature. I saw real dogs as I ran. They ripped my clothes and barked loudly as I ran for my life. The Boers keep angry dogs . . ."

Ebrahim defeats me. My prosecution is almost ended, and he shows me only the confused face of an illiterate. All that learning is like a candle in the wind, and it's all but blown out. I observe his torn and mud-spattered clothes, and I see no handsome gentleman there but a pariah. He's one of those filthy peasants of India, become an anonymous Untouchable from this location. The Brahmin Boers pursue this kind of vermin. I ask my final question:

"Did you see their leader?"

Ebrahim's eyes flicker and intelligence informs his face. The garments of the Untouchable fall away and my Italian boy gazes back at me. I have my evidence; he will provide me with the necessary information now.

"Yes, I can tell you. I do remember the leader of the *kommando*. He was a huge man, like a giant. He's got powerful hands, and crushes men like flies. He gallops across the veld, and he's the leader of the pack. I know him, because he tormented me, and accused me of rape. He insulted me here in this room."

"You identify the right man. You recognized Petrus Nel who brought you here, handcuffed, to my house. He made you howl like a dog. He's coming back tonight, and he wants to finish off the job. Run while you still can. Nel will be without mercy, so escape while there is time. Otherwise, you are finished. I'll try and help you."

Ebrahim hesitates, and I watch the confused emotions war within his personality. I see that the Kaffir warrior is fierce and powerful, while the insecure boy is confused and the Untouchable from the location cringes. He must not delay too long. Nel is after him, and he brings his pack.

"No. I'm staying. I'll hide anywhere. Help me find a place."

"Don't hesitate, because things have got worse. Sannie is pregnant."

He gasps and his anguish is apparent. His voice is a low moaning sound.

"No! No, it isn't true. I haven't fathered a child. I don't want to be responsible for another victim, another bastard from the location."

"It's true. You are the father of this child. Don't try and deny your paternity."

Ebrahim's expression alters, as his eyes dilate with anger. He possesses the resilience of a Kaffir warrior, and snarls angrily.

"They can keep the child. It's another black bastard, my memento to the Boers. A black warrior's seed fell in a white bed, and my child will flower in their midst, even though they hurl this son back into the location. The child will not forget.

Others will take up arms, and the Boers will suffer. They hunt me now, and I am their victim. This child changes things, for now I am the dorp's bastard son-in-law. I'll meet this *kommando*, and they will not intimidate me. I am their equal. Even though I'm a man without a gun, I'll still fight back."

He speaks brave words, but it's all useless now. The Boers will hunt him down and his only chance lies in escape. I shout:

"You seduced the Boer girl, and now you will father a bastard. You are the outcast, not me. The *kommando* want you. I'm a woman, and I'm safe from their anger. Run for your freedom, like an animal, otherwise it will be too late for either of us."

Ebrahim chooses to ignore my angry words. Instead, I see that his chemistry undergoes changes as desire suffuses his face, and his body becomes languid, and he is once again the seducer. He touches my cheek, with a delicate and tender touch. He again attempts to embrace me, and I find his aroused body desirable, yet I refuse to surrender to his warm animal attractiveness. Instead, I accept my own weakness and struggle like a mother who must still save her precious child. I speak, with all the common sense that I can muster.

"You must escape. The Boers must not humiliate you, and they have that power. Ugly men can break your body, and clever men can unhinge your mind. It must not happen."

He is a seducer, and importunate too. I remember too much about the sheer idolatry of love. There is no recapturing that original splendor of Sanjay's lips at my breast, and my own nakedness spilling like water. I cannot make the journey again, for I would blaspheme my own life. The past is unique, even in its pain and bitterness. The present life is futile. He offers me a tainted love. Lakshmi shimmers here, as if she had stepped down from the temple wall. She is free to entice here, and remains the eternal girl, who flows like a river. Sanjay floats like a corpse, as her silver necklaces jangle, and the ruby in her nose shines. The world is my child, and I know the many who are in need of love. I reject Ebrahim's ardor.

"You are a seducer . . . a liar. You will not exploit me. I am not the Boer girl. You debase love and abuse sex, and make it a criminal act. I despise you, and your weakness sickens me. Get out of my house and run for your life. I'll be safer without you."

Ebrahim does not flinch at my words. He sees this anger as a manifestation of passion, which it is. This is not carnal love, but rather the love of truth. It fills me now. It is the love that made Christ chase the money-lenders out of the temple. It is the love that forced Gandhi to become a revolutionary and lead others to their own salvation. This is the sesame seed that sprouts in my hands, and it's as if I hold a thousand-branched tree, and these hands of compassion stretch out and touch others. This is pure love, and it has nothing to do with sexual arousal, or blind selfishness. Ebrahim is not dismayed, but laughs and it's the snorting of a rutting animal or the braying of a donkey.

He remains and makes himself comfortable. He stretches out in a chair, and his keen eyes watch me. He's like an animal in the shadows. I whisper, more to myself than to this feckless boy.

"You are a foolish . . . stupid . . . ignorant child. You understand nothing. I tried to give you the world, the sesame seed of Gandhi and the pearl of the Medicis. You squandered it, and threw it away. Somehow, I am to blame. I am responsible too."

We wait now only for the arrival of the *kommando*. Ebrahim sleeps in his chair. The mirages flicker in the lamplight.

Kasturbai beckons and I follow her. She leads me across a desert. The city of Ahmedabad is distant and glows on the horizon. Pilgrims flock to Sabarmati. Gandhi addresses the multitude, and shares that dream of a classless society. He wears a white *dhoti*, and carries a staff. It's a rod of power, the trident of Shiva. He's a mahatma, a greatly holy one. Kasturbai squats near a pool. A sacred cow passes, and the animal drops its dung. Egrets fly above. Kasturbai fixes her gaze on the horizon, and I do the same. I abdicate too.

PART THREE

The Kommando

It's after midnight. I notice that Mars is still red in the sky. The planet warns of a revolutionary century, even though Gandhi spins at Sabarmati and Kasturbai stirs the pots. The maelstrom of events will continue: the aftermath of the Great War, the Bolshevik Revolution and the echoes of the Boer War. I'm glad that I was born a woman rather than a man.

There are sounds of horses pounding through the streets. I hear men's voices raised in anger. The *kommando* has arrived. Ebrahim is jolted out of sleep, like a lover thrown out of paradise. He shivers momentarily, and then jumps up and pushes a chair against the door. It's a futile exercise, and will not repulse the *kommando*. He asks:

"What shall we do?"

"We've got to open up."

I draw the bolt, and Ebrahim behaves like a pale and frightened child. I fling open the door and face the men, who now congregate on my doorstep. The night air is chill, and the houses gleam with an unexpected whiteness in the moonlight. The wind bends the fir trees. This *kommando* is no apparition. These men are flesh and blood. They are Boer officers and powerful adversaries. Each man carries a Mauser rifle and a bandolier that holds ammunition, and they wear those black claw-hammer coats and broad-brimmed hats. Some hold up lanterns. Petrus Nel is the undisputed leader. He points to Ebrahim, and issues an order:

"Take him."

The *kommando* moves forward like a single man. Their precision is astonishing. Ebrahim is already mobilized for flight. He looks toward the window, and finds his escape, as if one magnificent leap would give him a lifeline of freedom. The *kommando* anticipates this move, and blocks his movement. These men now guard all the strategic exits. My house is surrounded by Boers. I intercept and bar their way and insist:

"Where is your search warrant?"

Nel is officious, and answers with contempt.

"There isn't one, and it's not necessary. We are the authority here. You must stand aside, Juffrou. Surrender the Hottentot, and keep out of this matter. This is our business now, and men must settle it together."

I stand my ground, and refuse to be intimidated by this Boer pack of wild dogs. I answer severely.

"The boy is in my custody, and remains with me. You won't take him without a fight."

Nel hesitates, and dares not grapple with a woman. The *kommando* vacillates. I don't fear the cold steel of those Mausers. They can lift their rifles like a firing squad. The *kommando* can shoot down Ebrahim, and he can die like a dog in this room. They will not touch me because I'm a white woman and I'm saved by my skin color and my sex. I have the advantage. Impetuously, I wish that I were a black man. Then I would take on these Boers in physical combat. I examine the faces of the *kommando* and look for signs of remorse but find none. I recognize the men of the dorp: Andres Perreira, Charl Myburg, Jan Volschenk, Basie Viviers, Piet Burger, Wim Pieterse, Kobus le Grange, Ben Potgieter, Piet Barnard, Frans du Plessis, Willem Goosen and Petrus Nel. Everyone is present, and there is no dissenting voice. I speak to these acquaintances.

"We are neighbors, and are not at war. We need to talk about your grievances. I have a right to be heard too, so I suggest that we discuss the matter."

Petrus Nel's brief reply allows for no parley. He speaks in a brisk and determined manner.

"Our business is urgent. Just surrender the Hottentot. Time is short and you must do as we order. We do not want trouble, but must insist on justice."

Nel has not changed. He's still that warmonger, and the dorp's troublemaker. I appeal to Piet Burger in the hope that his might be the dissenting voice here.

"Meneer Burger, I need some advice. I want to plant some fruit trees, and I prefer peach. But plum would do. I love the blossoms. What do you advise?"

Piet Burger is a thick-set man, with confident and capable hands, and his fruit trees are the best. He knows good soil. His reply is affable and reticent:

"I'd recommend that you plant in July, which is the best month. Peach trees are difficult, and apple trees do better. It's our harsh climate. Look at the fir trees, and you'll understand that the wind lops off the branches, and the snow does its damage, too. The seasons test us, and we've no alternative but to plant carefully."

Piet Burger is a supporter, and gives nothing away, other than good advice. Yet his reserved manner hints at the fact that he has sided with this *kommando*. He can never be an ally, so instead I confront Charl Myburg:

"Meneer Myburg, you are a Greek scholar and I respect your learning. We have debated together and studied Plato, and I've even talked of Gandhi, and his non-violent philosophy of *ahimsa*. You know my views, and you also appreciate ethics. You cannot possibly agree with the motives of this *kommando*."

Charl Myburg does not flinch at my words. He has his own ideas about justice and answers.

"A crime was committed; a Boer girl was raped. Now she carries an illegitimate child, and it will be a Black baby. We will all suffer that stigma. This has got nothing to do with philosophy. Justice is necessary."

Charl Myburg fails me, and I recognize another trusted member of this *kommando*. I look out of the window. The moon rides the night sky, and she's like a woman who seeks a lover. This night is ravishing and death would be a crime, a blemish upon the earth. I know that Ebrahim is trapped, a buck caught in a snare. He struggles, and cannot pull free.

I turn to Andres Perreira. I believe in his decency, and that he cannot have sided with this *kommando*. I speak:

"Andres, you are different. You are Portuguese, and don't belong with this *kommando*. Africa is not your homeland, and you are not a member of the *volk*. You must still dream about Lisbon, with those balmy summer nights and sparkling wine. Don't give up that European heritage for this arid land and its own bitter truths. You are not like these other men."

"Miss Ransome, don't chastise me. I know that we talked and drank wine together. I do remember those gentle summers in Lisbon, and I know the interior gardens, with their unexpected coolness. I can never forget those nights filled with moths, and I long to return to Portugal, but it's just a dream. My survival is here in Africa, and I've bought my farm, and I need the support of this *kommando*. Try and understand my dilemma."

Andres Perreira disappoints me. His ancestry is Portuguese and he will always be an exile here, and I still refuse to believe that he's joined these thugs. I turn in desperation to the butcher, but I'm not hopeful, as I know that Jan Volschenk is a limited man. I say:

"Meneer Volschenk, I am one of your customers. You sell only choice cuts and your prices are fair; your meat is excellent. The *kommando* will not assist you with your business. These men are outlaws. You would be wiser to withdraw, and not support them in their evil errand here tonight."

The butcher's face is unshaven, and dark hairs line his wrists. His belly spills over his belt, while his fingers itch for the meat cleaver. He replies.

"Juffrou, you are a good customer. I give you only the best . . . prime mutton . . . tender chops . . . calf's liver. I never stint you.

But things are not always so simple, and a decision is often more difficult than quartering a sheep. A man alone cannot solve it. Twelve men are better. We are an unofficial jury, and God is our judge. We won't make a mistake, and our judgment will be fair."

The butcher is mistaken. Justice is not weighed on a scale like a pound of steak. I'm aware of the cost of justice, and it's not measured in pounds. It's got to do with men's hearts.

I take on Wim Pieterse next. His blue eyes are clouded, and he will surely not parry with clever words, but give me a straight answer.

"Meneer, I respect you. You are an honest man, and cannot agree with this *kommando* and their illegal methods. You must speak your mind now."

Wim Pieterse's mild eyes appraise me, and he searches my face as if seeking out my motive for this investigation. He knows that it involves more than just Ebrahim, and senses that it's got to do with my own morality, and the power of *ahimsa*. He speaks:

"A girl of this dorp was raped, and it's an ugly crime. You surely cannot condone it, yet you choose to protect the criminal. I find that hard to understand. I'm a valid member of this *kommando*, and I consider it a privilege. It's more than justice. We are guarding our heritage, and must think of future generations."

Wim Pieterse disappoints me. He'd be better off playing cards tonight. He's just another traitor. I face the other men who shuffle in embarrassment. Kobus le Grange speaks and declares himself a spokesman for the others.

"It's quite clear. We are a military tribunal, and have acted before during the Boer War, when times were also difficult. Then, Boer officers ordered traitors and spies to be executed. It's no different now. We are still the vigilant ones, and must remain prepared. We are still soldiers. The Hottentot must be punished, and it's our duty to dispense justice."

I no longer doubt that these men are committed, for they all support this *kommando*. Yet I find myself disgusted. They speak not only out of a righteousness, but also a grim retribution. They are without mercy, and I fear their intentions. One man has avoided me. I spy the lupine face and rangy body of Willem Goosen. He has no words and needs none, for he has other senses. He's already got the scent of the crime, as he sniffs out the victim and watches Ebrahim. He's the *kommando*'s watchdog. I rally my own energies and seize at a last chance. I insist on a moment's truce, and beg Nel for this favor.

"Meneer, it's indecently late. The *kommando* must be fair. I want a hearing, and I've got something to say. My evidence is important, so call off your men, and let the *kommando* wait outside. They intimidate us. I ask you to disarm, and put aside your gun. We are only a woman and a boy, and we have been tyrannized enough tonight. Don't refuse me this favor."

Nel pauses; he doesn't want to appear cowardly. He orders the *kommando* and they break ranks and spill out into the street. Nel remains alone, and reluctantly puts down his rifle and struggles out of his bandolier. He suddenly appears naked. But he still embodies the dangerous elements of a powerful warlord. He watches Ebrahim lurking in a corner and half-hidden by shadows. The boy bides his time; he'll choose his moment, and then strike. He'll uncoil and spit like the hooded cobra. Nel's vision extends like a web, and we are trapped there. He speaks:

"There's little to discuss. A white girl was raped, one of our own Boer daughters. You can understand our anger, as you are a woman too. Surrender the Hottentot. We don't want to shoot. We only want justice."

"Wait for the courts, and let them decide."

Nel angrily shakes his head, and will settle it now. He trusts only himself and this illegal *kommando*. He answers:

"I distrust liberal judges, and English-speaking juries are suspect. This is a crime against us all. One of our children has been outraged, and our dorp is threatened. This is our business, and we'll settle it now."

He is mistaken. This is a matter for the law. He is not a fair judge, and this *kommando* is no objective jury. I insist:

"Don't take the law into your own hands. You are ordinary citizens and none of you is impartial. You already judge Ebrahim, and find him guilty, yet you've heard no evidence. You are no worthy judge, and these other men are not a fit jury."

Nel pauses, and examines my face. He is withdrawn and bleakly objective as he puts my words to the test and replies with a newly found certainty.

"We have our credentials."

I am bewildered by his statement. I fail to understand how these soldiers, who know only about war, can now claim the right of jurists.

"I don't understand."

"We are Boer officers. We have all seen battle. None of us is a coward, and a few among our company are heroes. We've won our authority."

"I still don't understand. This is not a military matter. You are talking of war, and my house is not a battlefield. I grapple with justice too, and understand it differently. I see only the weak who need protection against the aggressors."

"We are judges, and we are a jury too. War empowers us, and we speak out of knowledge of death. We do not want to hunt this Hottentot. We want to try him, and impose our punishment. Allow us this opportunity, and hand over the prisoner."

"I refuse."

I will protect Ebrahim, who still stands within my circle of power. Gandhi's voice reverberates within me, and I wield Kasturbai's sword. Somehow, we will both endure this long night. Nel speaks in a somber tone.

"Then, we will testify. You will hear our evidence. Each man will recount his experience of battle, and you will not argue then. You will understand, and no longer question our authority."

I watch, confused, as Petrus Nel assumes power and grows

in stature. He is like the chorus of a tragic play, whose theme is battle, and I am forced to listen. Nel calls out a name, and I see a man step forward.

"Basie Viviers."

I recognize an old campaigner. Basie Viviers' face is like a map, and life's battles are written there. Pain is lodged inside his cranium as he remembers battle, and his bowels turn wetly.

"I fought at Majuba, and the battle cries still echo. I recall that we rode in and took the enemy by surprise. We were a *kommando* of over two hundred men. We fired from the saddle and the British Highlanders scattered. My horse reared and men were trampled under the hoofs. Our Boer attack succeeded, and we fought through to the British command post. I saw General Colley, who brandished a revolver, and fired again and again, but his magazine was empty. The British general was dazed and I could have killed him, but I refused, and allowed him to live. I'm no coward. Then, the demented British officers pushed past their general, as their army fled in defeat. I turned my attention to those fleeing Highlanders with their kilts flying like skirts. They all looked like women, and I laughed as I fired. These men dressed up in their skirts were shit-scared too, as they ran for their life. They were men from England going mad in Africa, and it was a ribald joke. Their bodies were ridiculous. One had a kilt over his head, but he didn't display any pantaloons, no ladies' drawers, no undressed delight. Instead there was just an ugly death. An absurd and funny war, but I don't laugh now. I ache, and I taste shit too. I'm down on all fours, and I'm eating earth, and I'm choking on that shit-filled and blood-stained earth of Majuba."

Basie Viviers steps back. He's not on four legs like an animal. He's a man, and he stands on both feet. He takes a sip of wine and rinses out his mouth. He spits and the wine is a vanishing red stain, like the spilled blood of Majuba. There is no forgetting this battle. Petrus Nel calls out another name.

"Piet Burger."

This man testifies now, and he's also caught up in the cycle of destruction that cuts down the victor and the vanquished alike. The Boer War and the Great War are both over, yet the dead remain, whether they are those kilted Highlanders or the dead of the Somme and Passchendaele. Piet Burger speaks:

"I was part of a Boer reconnaissance unit. It was early on in the war, and I was stationed near Pretoria. We rode out on a mission, and didn't expect any trouble. Then, we stumbled upon a British company. We looked down upon the enemy, and I watched them through field glasses. That was my first sight of the British. We were up on a hill and had the advantage, and they were easy targets. But I was unprepared for what I saw— the British officers had brought their wives and they picnicked as a band played gay tunes. I was bewildered. The women's presence made any attack seem like a violation. It was like an unnatural act, an aggression upon nature itself, man becoming more of a beast than even the animals. These thoughts passed rapidly through my mind. Our *kommandant* took his opportunity and ordered an attack. We rode in, and I did not even hesitate, as my reflexes were those of a man trained in warfare. I questioned nothing and killed in order to survive. We shot the officers first, and then dealt with the men. The women retreated into a wagon, and we ignored their screams. We won this skirmish, and then helped bury the dead. We also set up an emergency first-aid post, and men who had caused death now became stretcher-bearers and endeavored to save lives. We made bandages and we stemmed the flow of blood and cared for the injured. I dared not face the women, for I feared their accusing eyes. The image of the beast returned, and I convinced myself that I was doing a duty. It was a strange end to battle: women who cried, and men who died. I've tried to make some arithmetic out of the whole thing, but I fail to come up with any fair equation. Those hours waged in battle were like a descent into hell, and there was no hope of a redemption. I still don't understand it . . ."

Piet Burger is rightly confused. I need to ponder too. These images are close in feeling to the subjects of medieval artists— the Renaissance man, and the problem of sin. Petrus Nel is a surrogate Christ, and he carries within himself the arsenal of war, like wounds received upon a cross. He is also a Titan, and urges others to take on the travail of war. He is the greatest enigma of all. There is only one answer, Gandhi's doctrine of *ahimsa*, passive resistance. He is the Mahatma now, and Kasturbai fans him. Her eyes are compassionate. His lips frame a word . . . AHIMSA . . . I repeat it, and the sound of *ahimsa* is on my lips too.

Petrus Nel is oblivious to my mood. He is too absorbed, and plays his part as the chorus in this drama. He is the repository of violent intentions, and funereal as a character in a medieval mystery play. He reflects the dark Lenten draperies, and the urns of ashes, and is intent on his own mortification. I see only Gandhi, who spins a golden thread of truth, and it encircles the world, and I catch this thread of Gandhi's semen. It's been so hard to find, yet it's so finally there. I too possess that sesame seed, and divest myself of the dross, and my own selfishness. I strive after a real poverty of the spirit. I again whisper . . . *ahimsa* . . . *ahimsa*. Petrus Nel calls out another name.

"Willem Goosen."

I am taken aback. The lean and barely human Goosen circles me, as if I am his prey now. He is like a wolf, as he comes close and sniffs the hem of my dress. Soon, he will bay, and that will be an ugly sound. He circles me again, and then speaks.

"I watched, and I learned from what I saw. The Xhosa taught me, and the jackal too. I am his shadow. In the war, I crept up Schuinshoogte, and hid behind the *tambookie* grasses, and was another lion. My powerful heart beat, and I forgot that I was a man. It still happens to me, and the knowledge of just who I am fades, and this body drops away too. I can still sit in that silence. That day at Schuinshoogte, the lion took over. I charged through the *tambookie* grasses, and my knife was like a tooth.

I stabbed British soldiers, and I slaughtered them. They were warm inside like a young buck, and they had soft pelts too. I've almost forgotten the war. I only know that a thing lives, and then it dies. It's easy to understand."

Willem Goosen is still the lion, and the *tambookie* grasses hide him now. The silent stones clamor, and the bright-eyed lizard scuttles away. He's almost an endangered species, a white man who is also a primitive. He's been isolated, and the news of murder hasn't reached him. He'll stumble upon a story, and learn the lesson of Cain and Abel. Then, his guilt will be terrible. He'll lose that dangerous innocence, and become like other men. Petrus Nel calls out another name.

"Andres Perreira."

The tormented Andres Perreira steps forward. He whispers a prayer, and makes an ineffectual sign of the cross. He speaks of his part in battle.

"I am no Catholic even though my name is Perreira. I am like you all, and proved my courage at Elaandslaagte. It was a hard and desperate battle. We were camped on a hill, and watched the British maneuver on the plain beneath us. Then, a thunderstorm broke and torrential rain fell. The enemy was thrown into confusion, and a colonel shouted an order and the Manchester regiment advanced. This was our opportunity, and we opened fire. I pulled the trigger again and again and witnessed distant figures topple. They were insignificant as broken toys, and I accepted no responsibility. I reloaded and fired, and my innocence was stripped from me that day. I was barely nineteen, and I'd sold some part of myself at Elaandslaagte. War had raped me, and I was no longer a virgin in life. I was a mercenary, who plundered, and then moved on. I fought other battles, and finally came here and put my head and my hands to work on this farm. But it's all useless, for it seems as if I plunder the earth not only in war but also in peace. I steal from the snake in its hole, and filch from the nests of birds. I disturb the proliferation of the bush and its wild flowers. I desecrate life, and I remain a stranger here. I stand as a mercenary and fight for what is mine."

Andres Perreira weeps and is rightly unhappy. War is like a contagion which spreads and infects others. Nel interrupts and the spittle is fresh on his lips as he calls out another name.

"Piet Barnard."

Piet Barnard is grim-faced, as he too animates the battle of Elaandslaagte, and the ugly black smoke of war rises again like a pall over the Karoo. Piet Barnard speaks:

"Elaandslaagte! I agree that it was a terrible battle. I went through it too. I was with General Koch, and his party, and he led us in a last final ambush. We attacked General Hamilton and his men, and that was our mistake, because Hamilton managed to rally his company. A bugler sounded the call, and soon the Yorkshire regiment arrived with bared lances, and then a cavalry regiment joined them. We were outnumbered as these officers wielded sabers, and they carved us up. General Koch shouted a warning, but it was too late. We tried to flee but our Basuto ponies were no match for the heavier cavalry horses. I mounted and rode like hell, but a cavalry officer threw me to the ground and I lay there and pretended to be dead. Then, I crawled through the mud and slid like a worm on my belly. I discovered the body of General Koch, and he lay dead in the mud just like another worm. The rain of Elaandslaagte fell upon us, and the mud covered us, and we stank of it. It was also that stench of death. I never feel clean, not even now. I wash my hands, and scrub my nails. It doesn't help. God should speak and remind us not to kill . . ."

Piet Burger exposes pain, and war is like a disease for which there is no cure. It reaches epidemic proportions and then we are engulfed in carnage again. The Great War is just over, yet there's always a distant sound of gunfire. There's never a real truce, and there is this great need for a true disarmament, the embracing of non-violent passive resistance. Nel calls out another name.

"Wim Pieterse."

Wim Pieterse's face is lined, as if war has coarsened him, and marred those fine Dutch features. He's bloated now like the other Boers. He speaks:

"We entered Dundee, and that was our mistake. The British had secretly withdrawn in the night, and left everything: their abandoned equipment, empty tents, baggage, and even all their provisions. General Yule moved his company, and duped us. Our men were cold and hungry and their morale was low and the discipline was lax. Some of us behaved like drunken louts who looted and robbed. I'm ashamed to confess it, but that's the truth, and war brings out the worst in men. Our *kommandant* insisted on a chase, and I was among the first to leave. We were on the track of General Yule, and it was a hard journey. We crossed swollen rivers, and I waded waist high and held my rifle above my head. Another member of our party was washed away. He screamed and we threw him a rope, but he missed his grip, and the waters carried him away. He went under like a drowning man. Still the heavy rains persisted. We were red-eyed and penitent men, but we kept up our pursuit of General Yule. At night we heard the boom . . . boom . . . boom of General White's guns, holding off our Boer forces at Rietfontein. One of our horses sank in the mud, and we linked arms together for we feared that we might slip and disappear too. But all our efforts were useless. We were too late, and General Yule reached Lady-smith. The British had won, and there was no battle, only a long journey, and a small loss of life. I experienced sadness even though I had not killed men. I've never taken a life, and I don't even hunt in the veld. I've no wish to destroy. My role here is that of a juryman, and I won't pull the trigger even for this *kommando*."

War teaches its own terrible lessons. Petrus Nel, this dema-gogue and instigator of violence, betrays these men. The Loots-berg close in, and night settles here like a dark reptile. Ebrahim is held in occupied territory, and so am I. The dawn must rise. Nel calls out another name.

"Jan Volschenk."

I recognize the butcher. Flesh is his trade. He's in business here with those hands like slabs of raw meat, and that fleshy tongue which is so adept at perjury. He speaks now.

"Schuinshoogte! We surprised the British, and fresh-faced boys ran for their life. There were screams in the air, and the sound was worse than an abattoir. A young subaltern rushed toward me, and then fired, but his magazine was empty. He had blue eyes, and I don't regret sparing his life. A young calf must not be slaughtered too early, and lambs must be fattened up. Then you get good chops. War is the same. A mature man can face death, as do animals at the moment of slaughter. There's a wisdom to war; it's the great leveler."

I examine the corpulent butcher, with those hairy wrists that move slowly, and the fingers that run like spiders. He's not a lion in battle, but an even more dangerous animal. He's a man without a conscience. Nel calls out another name.

"Kobus le Grange."

Kobus le Grange has restless eyes. He knows how to appraise houses, yet he cannot assess the horrors of war. He speaks:

"Spion Kop! The flies attacked our dead. I remember those swarms of black buzzing flies as they settled on our corpses. Our morale was already low, and we felt that the war was now hopeless. The British were winning, and our Boer forces were pulling out. Men were saddling up and wagons were moving off, for the Boer army was in retreat. Then an exhausted horseman rode up, and this was none other than our new *kommandant*, General Louis Botha. His face was streaked with dirt, and his beard and hair were long. He had ridden for days, and did not dismount. He still sat on his horse and addressed us from the saddle. He reminded us of our birthright, and told us that we were the heirs to this beautiful land. We recognized ourselves as Afrikaners. He returned our burned farms to us, and resurrected our dead wives, and fertilized new hope in our lives. He urged us to defend Spion Kop. We dutifully accepted our task, and were prepared to defend this land, and would fight until death. I climbed the slopes again, and the stars seemed so close. Louis Botha was like an angel, who'd come in the darkness in the guise of a man, and showed us the stars again . . ."

Kobus le Grange's patriotism leaves me unmoved. The stars do shine but they are remote from our suffering. The moon peers with an inquisitive face, yet she too disdains our plight. The dogs howl as if they sense that something is wrong. The birds huddle in their nests and will be silent at dawn. No one can praise war, not even Louis Botha. Too much has happened since Spion Kop, for there's the Great War, and the Bolshevik Revolution, as well as other ugly incidents. These pustules of hate convince me that the battle never ends. Even now the *kommando* remains united, and none will defect. Nel calls out another name.

"Charl Myburg."

This scholar is a foolish elder who squanders his wisdom. His learning is a vanity, and he demeans poetry. He speaks:

"The Mauser rifle, the best there is. It's an extraordinary bullet, thin as a lead pencil, and drills a small hole in the skull and still misses the brain. Likewise the lungs. There's only a little bleeding, but no permanent damage. I marvel at this pathology. I envy the dead: they are better off than the living. I'm still dodging the bullet, even though the firing ceased long ago."

I disagree. There is no beauty in steel, and weapons are lethal. Nel senses my unspoken criticism and calls out another name.

"Frans du Plessis."

This man is deluded, as he holds the Mauser with respect. He should drop that gun, as if it were live coals. The weapon is dangerous: it can wound others, and even destroy its owner. The gun teaches pride and hatred, and is like a dangerous friend who is not to be trusted.

Frans du Plessis speaks:

"I agree that the Mauser is the best. I'm a locksmith and I recognize a good mechanism. The British used the Lee Enfield and it has its advantages. You must reload after each round.

Their cavalry officers favored the saber, but that was a mistake. We know better. Our experience of the Kaffir Wars taught us otherwise. An *assegai* is a raw blade too. Never trust a Zulu either. We still carry those old scars. A good gun is like a fine lock, and must be oiled and cleaned. The Mauser is a friend that won't let you down, and, unlike a woman, it's always faithful."

This talk of weapons sickens me. Gandhi carries only a staff, the trident of Shiva. He fears that his footsteps disrupt the life of insects. He is holy and even his shadow blesses all. His very breath can still the unruly hearts of others, and his compassionate glance releases men from their suffering. Gandhi is far away. He crosses India and Kasturbai follows him. She is his long, loping shadow and they travel together. He inspires me now, and I can sense his presence in this very room. I recall his image; that frame of bone and sinew; skin that has a dark patina; a skull that was a crinkled walnut; and then a warm handshake and a shy smile. I have recreated Gandhi here, even though he's trekked elsewhere. He's found other "children of God," and Brahmin Boer and Coloured Untouchable are not among his classless society. The revolution will still take place. The anger of this knowledge resounds in me. I wait for the red light of dawn to streak the sky, and the birds will be ungagged then, and will celebrate the day.

Ebrahim prowls like a nocturnal animal, and I don't underestimate him. He is made strong by the darkness. Only I am weakened by the night and need the sun to rise. Nel calls out another name.

"Ben Potgieter."

The engineer steps forward, and he is the architect of order. He visualizes roads and bridges that will span the Karoo and link us to civilization. He can tunnel through mountains and dam rivers. He speaks:

"I agree, and I despise the lance. We Boers were never a trained army. Our real ally was the veld, and the British were lost there. We took our advantage. Every Boer soldier was his own general, and it's still true. We are self-sufficient, and our errand tonight proves it."

Ben Potgieter is the last to speak. Petrus Nel is the only man left now. He wears the expression of a religious zealot, and I am again reminded of those faces seen in medieval paintings, a tortured Christ, or a proud Titan. I read the travail of suffering on his face. He speaks now as if war is a crusade, a holy journey on which some evil is met and then routed. He speaks:

"Siege! I know all about it. Attack is often a mistake. I learned this lesson at Ladysmith. We had our artillery there, the howitzers and the Long Tom gun. It was our strategy that was weak. Our Boer leaders blundered, and insisted on an attack, and the British repulsed us. General Hamilton rallied his men, and the infantry charged with bare bayonets, and carved us up. I remembered our battles with the Kaffirs, and their *assegais*, that terror of the naked blade. We were in retreat, and it was a terrible day. God was against us too, and allowed a hailstorm to break. The hailstones were the size of pigeons' eggs and I saw men with cracked skulls. Then, there was still worse to come as the hailstones filled up the *dongas*, and the streams rose. There were sudden floods, and I saw men drown in front of my eyes. Few of us returned to our Boer lines, and we had lost the advantage. General Buller relieved Ladysmith, and so the British won. I've never recovered. Our Boer generals blundered, and should never have attacked. They should have waited, and I'd have grown old waiting too. The siege would have succeeded. The British would have diminished. Disease would have wracked them. Feeble-minded and dim men would have straggled out of Ladysmith. It would have been a Boer victory. Yet our generals blundered and failed the people. It will not happen now, and we will win this battle. Surrender the Hottentot . . ."

Ebrahim makes a leap, and he is the sure-footed lion. His claws are extended. He wears the merciless smile of a warrior, as he lunges and snatches up Nel's rifle and bandolier. Nel regrets that he agreed to disarm, and remembers how he left the gun propped against a chair. Ebrahim holds this prize now. The men of the *kommando* are jittery, and raise their rifles. I scream:

"Hold your fire!"

They press forward. They are angry and confused men, and they throng into my house like an invading army. They are the new Goths and Vandals, and will ransack my home. They will destroy law and order. Civilization is in ruins, and we move into a dark age. I face ugly men, as Jan Volschenk holds me within his sights. Piet Barnard screams profanities. Basie Viviers takes aim, and Ebrahim is the quarry now. Petrus Nel shouts an order.

"Hold your fire. The Hottentot must surrender. Leave it to me."

The situation has altered, and Ebrahim has won bargaining power. He holds the gun. He has grown huge. Within seconds, he assumes the form of a Kaffir warrior, and Moselikatse's blood pounds in his veins. He doesn't tremble, but matches the gun's aggression. He emerges from a dark continent, and sees the Boers as white invaders who have fallen within his sights. He has but a single task, the destruction of this enemy. He shouts:

"Stand back, Boers. Be careful now; I have the gun. It's mine and I'll shoot."

Nel replies with a chilling persuasiveness. He is like a man pacifying a wild animal.

"Give me the gun."

Ebrahim laughs, and it's a rattling hyena sound. He smiles and displays white teeth, and answers aggressively.

"No. The gun is mine, and works for me now. It's become my tame gun, and will turn on its Boer masters. Nel, get out of here. Turn your pack of wild dogs loose in the veld. I'll be out hunting tonight."

The situation is dangerous, and Ebrahim must be reasonable. I try with my own plea, in the hope of reaching him, as I say:

"Ebrahim, please return the gun. It doesn't belong to you.

This is a dangerous weapon, and we could all get hurt. This is ugly behavior."

He brings the power of an *impi* into the room. Feathers would look resplendent in his hair, and copper bracelets would show off his strong arms. He ignores my plea. Petrus Nel is wary. He's middle-aged but still agile, and an experienced tracker. He has his own instincts of survival. He charges Ebrahim and attempts to retrieve the gun, but the warrior is ready. Ebrahim retaliates and jabs the rifle butt into Nel's guts. The Boer hits the floor, and I half expect to see Ebrahim execute a war dance, or give a battle cry. He does neither. Instead, he kicks the prone body of the Boer, and Nel lets out a low moan of pain. Ebrahim gives that rattling hyena laugh.

The *kommando* are stunned. They are angry and raise their rifles. This time, they will shoot. Nel rises gingerly and wipes the dust off his clothes, and limps toward the *kommando*. They stare at him in disbelief and fear the worst. Nel is ashen-faced, but he is still the clever general and faces his men squarely. He reveals his strategy.

"Listen to me. Forget this humiliation, and learn from Ladysmith. Attack is a mistake, so put down your rifles. War involves strategy. We are not outlaws. We are Boer officers, and we do not shoot a man down like a dog, or a jackal. I am ready to deal fairly with the Hottentot. He must surrender immediately, otherwise, we will begin the siege, and then he will not last the night. I'm certain of it. This plan assures us of victory."

The *kommando* breaks ranks, and the men talk among themselves. They allow Nel time to deliver the ultimatum. Basie Viviers is upset. He disagrees and rages and could suffer a stroke. The others are in agreement. Ben Potgieter takes a stroll, and seeks a moment's solitude. Piet Burger fumbles for tobacco, as smoking calms him. Andres Perreira whispers a Catholic prayer, and Charl Myburg quotes a Greek quatrain. Jan Volschenk contemplates quartering a sheep. Kobus le Grange examines a house, and knows how to profit from a quick sale. Wim Pieterse whistles, and Frans du Plessis jangles his bunch of keys. Piet Barnard looks at the stars, and Willem Goosen dreams of the veld. Petrus Nel delivers the ultimatum. He shouts:

"Hottentot! Surrender immediately. We will surround the house. Come out now, with your hands up. There is no escape. We will block every exit."

Ebrahim laughs, and he is once again the hyena, who snarls and threatens with the gun.

"Boer! I won't miss this time. Just call off your pack of wolves."

"Jackal."

Nel is contemptuous and sees Ebrahim as vermin. He makes one last effort, and chooses me as the mediator.

"Juffrou, we don't want a fight, and you can help us. Try and make him surrender. It's for his own good. There's no sense in killing him."

Nel is right. This berserk youth is also my gifted pupil. I try and remember this as I resurrect my faith in the Italian boy and say:

"Ebrahim! You are like my own son. End this madness. You cannot win against the Boers. Return the gun to Mr. Nel, and you will be treated fairly."

Ebrahim laughs, and it's like the rattle of machine-gun fire. His teeth gleam with an animal whiteness. They are like sharp weapons. He holds up the gun, as if it were a trophy, and shouts:

"Be careful, Boer. The gun is mine now, and I'm the one in power. I'll never surrender."

His vain play-acting finally defeats me, and I'm forced to speak angrily. He plays such dangerous games, and he's also guilty. He seduced the Boer child and he must pay a price. Lakshmi shimmers here a moment. She glides past on delicate feet, the eternal girl, who is like a river, the most perfect of all children. She is a Tantric goddess, Kali, the destroyer, and I refuse to be subjugated. All children must grow up. There are no more games, and all fantasies must end. I speak:

"Ebrahim, face the truth. Give up this play-acting. None of it is real. There is no Italian boy. It's all make-believe. Pompeii and Florence are in ruins, and the museums of Italy are empty. The war has closed them. Your dreams are a fraud, and you'll never travel anywhere. You belong in the Karoo. The lover is a fake, a seducer, who abuses women. You must seek love elsewhere. Journey to India, and go to Sabarmati. Find the *ashram*, and Gandhi is there. You'll recognize him, as he wears the white *dhoti*, and carries a staff, the trident of Shiva. Kasturbai is his regent, and she is fearless. Trust her with your sorrow, and she'll bring you balm. These are your friends. Examine the men of the *kommando*. They are warriors too. Witness their hands that carry death, and know that they are men matured in gun-fire. They already pollute you, now that you hold one of their guns. Don't imitate them, but live in the light of your own beauty."

Ebrahim is appalled at my outburst, and holds the gun up like a Kaffir shield, as if trying to ward off my words. This outburst is another kind of gun-fire, and he's shattered, and must muster his own energies. He replies:

"Try and understand that the gun protects my freedom. I won't give it up and I cannot surrender. Nel is strong and threatens me. My life is at risk, and the gun looks after me. I will not be a caged animal, and no prison will hold me. I suffered there, and the warders cut my hair, and mocked my manhood. They despised my color. The *kommando* is no different. I'm holding onto the gun, and I will defend myself. The Boers won't destroy me, and their huge hands won't crush me. I am not a fly in their web. I've nothing to fear. I've got the gun, and I will never surrender."

Ebrahim glowers at Nel, and drubs on the floor with the rifle butt. He hammers out a furious tattoo, and it's a rallying cry. He musters new energies and Nel recognizes the truth. There will be no surrender. He speaks:

"Juffrou, this is useless talk. He's a dangerous animal and we must shoot. Please leave the house, and let me escort you to safety. He'll die here like a jackal, and we'll kick over his carcass in the morning."

I sob openly: my house is under siege. Nel is the clever strategist and the experienced general. He's been through this before, and he's learned from the siege of Ladysmith. Now he uses these tactics again, and I must sit it out. Ebrahim needs my help, and I cannot leave him. I will try and restrain this madman. The siege will not last the night. Nel has given us up, and has rejoined the *kommando*. The trouble is just beginning.

Men regroup in the darkness and words float across in the crisp night air. The Lootsberg rise up, and they are crystal towers. Gandhi must ring that mountain gong and liberate me from this moment. Snow is a white halo there. I hear a voice shatter the night. The word is *"Dynamite."* It sounds like Jan Volschenk's suggestion. I fear that they will blow us up. I catch another phrase. Piet Barnard speaks earnestly, and has another suggestion; *"We must smoke them out like rats."* Then, Andres Perreira cries out in a high falsetto voice: *"Mother of God, be merciful."* The voices fade and become conspiratorial whispers. We will not leave this house alive. The threat of siege hammers in my brain, and they will isolate us. Snipers will finish us off, or they will drive us mad. We are flies on a wall. The Mauser's appetite for death. Ebrahim watches me. His hair is a dark stubble, and the curls are gone. His eyes are bloodshot, and his hands tremble. His mind crawls now, as he oscillates between elation and despair. He alternates both as hunter and prey. He hesitates a moment, and then speaks:

"Will they shoot?"

"Does it matter?"

He suddenly laughs, and it's that rattling hyena sound which again begins to unnerve me. I suspect his intentions, as he makes another suggestion.

"I've thought of a new strategy. The Boers won't win, and they will not succeed with this siege. I have an idea that can save us."

"Forget it."

My reply is cynical. I'm not even curious, as I know that we will not last out the night. He grasps my hands and presses kisses on my wrist, and whispers urgently in a loving tone of voice.

"Listen to me: you will be my hostage. The Boers won't dare shoot a woman. Let them play at this siege, and we'll hold them off. We'll enjoy a honeymoon together. You will be my bride today, and I'll show you paradise."

His idea is crazy, and he's most certainly a madman. I am no hostage, and I will not die in a shoot-out, even for love. He must surrender. That's his only chance. I plead:

"Fool! You cannot hope to succeed. The Boers won't even listen. I am not a hostage. I'm a revolutionary woman, and the Boers will be glad to be rid of me. The *kommando* will shoot, and we'll both die like rats. Come with me, and hold my hand. We'll walk out into the street together."

Ebrahim clenches his fists. He wears the mask of an implacable warrior, and lifts the gun and aims the weapon at me. He is truly without mercy as he explodes into violent language.

"Shut up! You are my hostage. Do what you are told. I'll never surrender. Don't scream, or I'll shoot. It's your life, or mine. The *kommando* will understand."

The *kommando* maneuvers outside. Marksmen move in the shadows, and voices are raised. We are their targets. Nel steps forward and issues a final warning:

"Come out, and I mean both of you. Lift up your hands, and walk out into the street. Our marksmen are ready and in position. The house is surrounded. Surrender immediately, or you will die together. This is a last warning. Come out before it's too late."

Ebrahim trembles, and his face is ashen, as he curses: "*Fuck the bastards.*" Then, he overpowers me. I wrestle with this warrior with the hard muscles, and rough chin, and cold eyes. There is no love in any of this, yet his thighs bear down upon me. His feverish heartbeat pounds, as his hands ransack my breast. This is no consummation between lovers but a Vandal attempting rape. Ebrahim makes his own survival bid. I've become a thing, something to be used, abused and then abandoned. The rape of all women throughout history. Greeks, Goths and Vandals and every type of warrior perpetrated this crime. It's happening now, and it will go on. The toll of all women who are brutalized by men in their anger and their greed. I sink my teeth into his flesh and he howls like an animal. He attempts to push his fist into my face as I fight free. Then he gasps:

"Christina, I didn't mean it. I still love you . . ."

I weep silent and recriminatory tears. He sobs on my breast and whimpers like an upset child. This moment can never be recanted, and must be transcended. I try and soothe him. A mother cannot reject her terrible offspring. He pushes open the window. He again musters his energies and holds the rifle to my head. We are both play-acting now, the hunter and the prey; the mother and the son; the lover and his beloved. Ebrahim shouts:

"Stand back, Boer. I have a hostage, the English lady, Miss Ransome. If you shoot, she will die. Withdraw your marksmen."

The ruse succeeds, as Nel gestures to the marksmen and they withdraw. Angry voices are raised. The *kommando* is outraged. Basie Viviers shakes a fist and shouts: *"The woman is a bitch. She's a British spy. Shoot her."* Piet Barnard angrily agrees: *"She's a whore too, and a kaffir-boetie."* Jan Volschenk calls from the opposite house: he's one of the marksmen placed there, and he now shouts a warning: *"We will shoot. This battle will have its casualties."* Andres Perreira screams in anguish: *"Holy mother of God, forgive us!"* Wim Pieterse raises his voice and makes a plea for moderation: *"We must withdraw. The hostage situation changes things."* Nel advances unarmed. He's more like an oracle than a soldier, as he speaks:

"Hold your fire. The siege will begin. Thirst comes first, and then hunger, and that's only the beginning. It's not just the physical discomfort; there's also the terror inside a man. The nerve cracks and the will fails. Then even one's sanity is threatened. Victory is close for us. Ladysmith should have been ours, and our Boer generals blundered. We lost the war, but we'll win this skirmish. The siege will be short, and will not last the night."

I look into Ebrahim's anguished face, and he's a pale and fragile boy. Saliva flecks his lips and his eyes are somber. He puts a distance between us, and I cannot guess his intentions. He smiles, and his mouth is no longer sensual, but the lips are ascetic, like a curved blade. The assassins move closer, and Nel shouts an order. The *kommando* have become shadows, and fill the darkness. The night's tragedy proceeds, as Nel orchestrates the scenes. He is the perfect chorus. A hail of bullets could wipe us out, for we are the targets set up for death.

Ebrahim lifts the rifles, and it's more like a ritual implement, some ceremonial object from a temple, a trident of Shiva. He aims the gun at me, and I fall within its sight. I stand speechless, as he insists:

"Christina! I will shoot this time, and I'm not bluffing. We will die together in a suicide pact. You will go first, and I will follow. It's better this way. I have no life without you. I only wish that you felt the same way."

I don't believe in any cosmic copulation. There is no life for us together in some celestial realm. He's gone too far, and his words are just fireworks. He hasn't got any real guts, and won't pull the trigger. I answer:

"Ebrahim, this is useless talk, and it's all nonsense. The gun is ineffectual, an impotent weapon. You won't dare use it. I fear the guns of the *kommando*; they are the enemy. I've made up my mind too. I won't die in a shoot-out. I value my life and I'd betray myself if I stayed. I'm going out into the street. Come with me. It's still not too late. Hold my hand and we'll walk out together. There's still a chance."

Ebrahim smiles weakly, and his face holds a cloying smile. He relaxes his grip on the rifle and renders the weapon impotent as he chooses not to fire. Instead, he says:

"I didn't mean to shoot . . ."

"I see. Just another game."

He is unexpectedly calm. He quickly gathers in his powers, and the warring fragments come together. He cleaves together as a new person, and speaks with an urgency:

"Please, Christina, you must listen to me. It's important that you understand. I do love you. There's no doubt in my heart. There's a light in you, and it's more than just flesh. It's got to do with your own powerful energies. You have the power to resurrect others. You brought me back to life, and I am that Italian boy. He is not dead, and I speak with his voice now. Love is mysterious. I don't understand it, and I don't think you do either. There is no explanation. We are meant to be together. We are one like fruit on a tree. We are like minds as a river flowing. Our love will endure. The rest of the world is ignorant, and we both know it. The Boers are no longer real, and they have receded. This is our secret, and this knowledge eludes others. Resurrection is extraordinary."

I remain, and the power of his voice is insistent. Ebrahim has claimed his manhood. He is no longer the black warrior, nor is he the seducer, or that abused Untouchable. His is a passionate voice which belongs among the nineteenth-century Romantics. He has no connection with this revolutionary age. He presses kisses on my hand. Then, he takes up the rifle, and I again see the trident, the transforming rod of Shiva, the sexual power, and the life force. I understand his intention, but I am powerless to save him. He has removed me from the dangerous areas of his life. He speaks with shining eyes:

"Everything is meaningless. The *kommando* is outside. Grown men play at being soldiers, and it's a dangerous charade. We are all trapped, and none of us can escape it. The darkness is everywhere. The snipers won't succeed and the general's strategy will fail. Love is a lost cause, and the grave holds its secrets. There's nothing left."

I watch in hypnotic silence. Ebrahim raises the gun, that trident of Shiva. His body is a chimera. He caresses the barrel, and the Mauser is his obedient servant. He is a chaste partner.

A shot rings out, and he falls like a comet and blood spurts as a fiery tail. It flows like a river here and nothing can stem it. I bend over his torso, and he's become an overturned statue. The Vandals have invaded and the hero is dead. I cradle the child of love in my arms. The moon is at the window, and she is a voyeur, an obscenity in the sky. I weep and talk to this blood-splattered body:

"You are devoured! You've been eaten by your own entrails. Try and reshape yourself. Begin the birth process again. See yourself as a fish, and fly as a bird, and hunt like an animal. Then, you can return as a man. You will begin anew. You named it love instead of life and that was your mistake. You cheated and were dazzled by the trappings of love: the naked look and the power of one body pitted against another; the damp hair beneath a kiss; those taut muscles of a thigh; the soft white breast; the tongue and its wetness; the phallic power; the orgasm, that fall into nothingness. You've been tricked. There are no more reflections. The sea is empty. The fire is out. The sky is dead. Gandhi spins at Sabarmati, and his semen breeds the *satyagraha*. They are the lovers. The bed is the world, and everyone is a concubine. I tried to tell you this, but you refused to listen."

The bonds loosen, and I begin to understand. Ebrahim is gone. He's all in pieces, and so is my own life. Still, I am learning. Lakshmi is no temple goddess. She isn't a profane effigy, and adorns no temple wall. Instead she's a victim. She's been used. She's an object of abuse too, and she isn't the first. History tells of many others; those Chinese women with bound feet, and black women mutilated in tribal rites, and these Indian women. They are the child-brides in revolt: Ayesha Padaychee and her struggle. She fought against a Hindu father, and won her literacy. Zarina Cassim won her battle too. She was married by proxy in the city of Allahabad, and was shrouded in the Muslim *burghan*, so that no man could look upon her face. She too made her escape, and found a meaning in prison. Detention was no worse than marriage. The list is long, and the victims are many: Kasturbai, and her holy lord. She sits behind Gandhi, and fans him at meals. She is a thin, silent figure, the mother of an *ashram*. She is his shadow, the other side of his mind. She moves slowly, as if she knows that there will be a reckoning. Her own death brings its release. I am there too, and I touch the body of Sanjay, as he springs to life. His nakedness gleams, as he caresses me. The Natal beach is white moonlight. The moment is ecstatic. The sea buffets us and his form disintegrates. I hold only a thigh-bone, the palm of his hand, an ear like a scallop shell; toes that are starfish, a mouth that is an empty sea-urchin shell. I am holding the bones of love: the flesh is gone, it's been devoured. Gandhi cooks these useless bones and it will be soup for the *ashram* and ghee for Shiva's temple. A learning at last about usefulness. Love and its progression. The stages of the heart.

All these voices fill the house. The hundred thoughts of myself speak. The figments dance before my eyes: Lakshmi and her sadness; Kasturbai moving across India, a shadow that follows Gandhi; Zarina Cassim weeping by the Jumna River; Ayesha Padaychee studying an English dictionary. Sanjay walks with me along the beach. The mango trees are distant. The palm tree is like a tower. The sea is cool and refreshing and the water is soothing, like milk. There's no cloud on the horizon; it's a day full of light. I was so secure.

Ebrahim's head lies in my lap, with those soft lustrous eyes and his olive skin. Those perfect good looks. I share his dream of happiness. I too remember Europe, and know those lakes and forests. Now everything is shattered. An invading army rapes my mind. Abraham de Loor interrupts these thoughts, and the pressure of his warm and insistent hand says that I must reclaim my life.

"Come, Christina, it's time to leave. Don't clutch at these useless memories. You must let it all go. The Coloured boy is dead, and now you are free to leave New Kimberly."

Abraham de Loor's face is so old, like a piece of parchment. I imagine that ancient texts are written there, and he belongs to a people who have survived flood and persecution, as well as drought. He too has a life and feels and struggles to know. Still, I cry out my own despair.

"What is so wrong? Why is my life a mess? I thought I'd found it, that sesame seed, which was Gandhi's gift to me. There was a renounced life here, and I strove after humility and simplicity. It's like tissue paper and the wind has torn it to shreds. It's all over now. It was so delicate, a gossamer truth, and it's broken now like a spider's web. It's fallen apart."

Abraham de Loor touches my arm gently. Men come in and remove Ebrahim's body, and carry him with a detached indifference. He should be carried out on a bier. He was a prince. Nobody notices anything now. The dead are just dead, and the living are neglected too. The trees outside breathe, and the passion of the land rests in night. The Lootsberg mountains are dark silent towers. Abraham de Loor speaks:

"Christina, come with me. Don't talk any more. Don't torment yourself; it's finished now. Your visit to the Karoo is over. You are a survivor."

"A survivor, Braam. I don't know . . ."

I do not argue. My outburst is finished. I am dry inside. I am like wood that crackles in a fire and now sputters into a burning brightness. There's a sudden sharp pain, and then it's over. My anger is like that, and I've a sense of grief and a need for some redress. The list of victims grows. There are women in all circumstances, and there is no special age and no reason for this abuse. Women are women and men are men. The roles are too sharply defined. Some men are masters, few women are slaves. I try and heal myself. I dwell upon Gandhi's face in repose, and hear him again read from the Hindu scriptures. He talks of work as a holy task, and speaks of the joy of serving others. Then, I see Kasturbai bring the tea, and her strong arms serve food. Ayesha Padaychee sews by candlelight, while Zarina Cassim nurses a child. Sanjay shares my life. Ebrahim talks of Geneva. Abraham de Loor praises the Lootsberg.

My neighbors have a life too, and their work in the world goes on. Basie Viviers sits on his *stoep*. Piet Burger tends his fruit trees, and the war hasn't devastated them. Willem Goosen tends his flock, and sees the new lambs. Andres Perreira drinks wine and still dreams of Lisbon. Piet Barnard rolls up his sleeves and delivers a calf. Wim Pieterse saddles a horse and rides across his lands. Jan Volschenk quarters a sheep; the meat on his cleaver is clean. Kobus le Grange appraises houses and looks for a good buy. Charl Myburg improves his Greek, while Frans du Plessis fits new locks. Ben Potgieter erects a dam, and imagines a new road that will link New Kimberly with Graaff-Reniet and then the dorp will no longer be isolated. Petrus Nel is a soldier, and waits for trouble. He will sound the alarm, and the war will begin again.

Abraham de Loor takes my arm. He steers me and we walk through the ranks of the *kommando*. The moon is full, and she is no longer a voyeur. She is the queen of the night, and shines now with a resplendent indifference here. We walk beneath that light, and I recognize the men of the *kommando*. Their horses are tethered and they neigh softly, like beasts ready to plunge back into the caverns of the underworld. The moon reveals these Boer soldiers, and they are ominous in their knowledge of death. These are the messengers of the underworld. They guard the terrible mythology of war, and perform their rituals of retribution and death. I am free, and I've broken out of the dark kingdom. I address these men:

"Ebrahim killed himself, so the jackal escaped, the vermin eluded you. He fought like a man, and died in a war. He was as brave as any Boer. Don't think you've won, because nothing has changed. The war has stopped and the funeral will soon be over. The revolution goes on. Gandhi walks at Sabarmati, and wears brown sandals. He's dressed in a white *dhoti*, and carries a staff, that trident, Shiva's rod of power. He sows his sesame seeds. He is a father and also a creator. Gandhi's tears wet the world, and they will fall here as rain. Then, the drought in men's hearts will be over, and we will see a different society. There will be no Brahmins in their splendor, and no Untouchables in their poverty. I mean that we shall see no Boer enclaves, and no Coloured locations. I believe that such a classless society is possible in South Africa. This is the only revolution, and it is possible in this century."

Petrus Nel is indifferent. His appetite for war is limitless. It's as if he suffers a cancer, and must be devoured by his own pain. Yet, he is part of history too. He's one of the Goths and Vandals and leads this invasion. These same thugs sacked ancient Greece and Rome, and overturned statues and destroyed libraries. They also ransacked the medieval monasteries. These are the barbarians. These are the thugs and strong-men of history, and they are back with us again. The koppies are distant sentinels. New Kimberly is a last outpost and now the Karoo has been invaded. Nel speaks:

"You are a woman. We are men and know what is best. This is our land. We have defended it against the Kaffir hordes and the British, and we will repulse any army that threatens us. We are like Moses. We travel always through the Red Sea and Jehovah parts the waves and blesses our harsh trek. We cannot ever allow evil to sweep in off the horizon, and wars must be fought. We are ever-vigilant, and there is no rest for us. We are always prepared for trouble."

There is nothing left to say. The sky is flushed with a crimson light and orange glows there, and there are golden bands. But the colors of this dawn are predominantly red. This is a time of revolution. I mourn for this poor and blighted century. The sun is white, like a mirror of brightness. The Lootsberg rise up like pristine towers. Gandhi will ring that gong, and he will summon me again. Ebrahim tried to climb, and I failed to lead him to the summit. He tried to fly and fell out of the sky. He burned himself out. The ashes blow about. Nothing else remains. That's the tragedy. There is no handprint; no ocher stain; no fragmented rock painting; no femur; no early ancestor. I stretch out my empty hands. I weep because I hold nothing.

GLOSSARY

AFRIKANER CATTLE breed of cattle

AHIMSA the Hindu virtue of nonviolence, as epitomized by nonviolent passive resistance

ASSEGAI spear used by the Blacks in defending the territories

BASUTO PONY small African pony used by the Boers in warfare

BOESMAN derogatory South African name for a Coloured person

BRAHMIN member of the highest priestly Indian caste

BURGHAN veil which shrouds the features of a Muslim woman so that no man other than her husband can look upon her face

BYWONER poor white, an authorized squatter who works another man's land

CALABASH gourd used by Africans as a receptacle

CAPIE derogatory name for a Coloured person originally from the old Cape Colony

COLOURED South African name for a person of mixed blood or descent

DONGA dry eroded watercourse which runs only in times of heavy rain

DORP Afrikaans name for village

DRIFT shallow fordable point in a river, often where it crosses a road

GANESH the Hindu elephant-headed god

GARUDA BIRD the divine bird, half man, connected with the Hindu god Vishnu

GHEE paste applied to the lingam (phallus) as a mark of reverence in certain Hindu temples

HANUMAN the Hindu monkey-faced god, adept at scholarship

HOT-NOT, HOTTENTOT derogatory South African name for a Coloured person

IMPI battle formation used by Black tribes in their attacks on White settlers

INDENTURED LABORERS (INDIAN) Indian immigrants who came to Natal in South Africa in the late nineteenth century and worked under contract, for a pittance

JUFFROU Afrikaans term for an unmarried woman; also means "miss"

KAFFIR-BOETIE derogatory South African term for a white liberal

KALI wrathful Hindu goddess, who destroys ignorance and sin

KAPPIE large sunbonnet worn by Boer women

KAROO, THE semi-desert region of South Africa

KIST wooden chest used for household linens

KOMMANDANT senior Boer officer

KOMMANDO Boer military unit

KOPPIE, KOPJE small hill

LAAGER initially a Boer formation of wagons enclosing men and women and their posessions against Blacks' attack; also any refuge for Whites against a Black threat, especially in South Africa

LINGAM in Hinduism, a phallus, worshiped as a symbol of the god Shiva

LOCATION a segregated area in South Africa on the outskirts of a town or village, set aside for Blacks or Coloureds

MAYA the illusory nature of the world as explained in Hindu philosophy

MERINO breed of sheep

MOSELIKATSE a famed warrior chief of the Matabele

NAGA SERPENTS those of Hindu mythology who guard wisdom

NAWAB an Indian deputy ruler

VAN RIEBEECK, JAN first Dutch governor of the Cape, who arrived in 1648

SATYAGRAHA name given to Gandhi's passive resistance movement, both in South Africa and India

SJAMBOK stout rhinoceros or hippopotamus hide whip

SPRINGBOK antelope native to South Africa

STOEP Afrikaans word for verandah or porch

TAMBOOKIE kind of tall African grass

UNTOUCHABLE member of the lowest Indian caste, often considered a pariah

VEREENIGING, TREATY OF   treaty between the Boers and the British
   which ended the hostilities of the Boer War
VOLK, THE   "the Afrikaans people" of South Africa
XHOSA   the African people from the borders of the old Cape Colony
YONI   symbol of the female organ of generation, an object of ven-
   eration among Hindus